An Unnatural Life

ALSO BY ERIN K. WAGNER

The Green and Growing

AN UNNATURAL LIFE

ERIN K. WAGNER

A TOM DOHERTY ASSOCIATES BOOK

NEW YORK

AN UNNATURAL LIFE

Copyright © 2020 by Erin K. Wagner

All rights reserved.

Cover art by Will Staehle

Edited by Lee Harris

A Tordotcom Book
Published by Tom Doherty Associates
120 Broadway
New York, NY 10271

www.tor.com

Tor® is a registered trademark of
Macmillan Publishing Group, LLC.

ISBN 978-1-250-75208-6 (ebook)
ISBN 978-1-250-75209-3 (trade paperback)

First Edition: September 2020

For Andrew, who reads everything

A day on Europa is equivalent to 3.5 days on Earth. The lifetime of a *robotnik* is equivalent to two human lifetimes.

> It is in the judgment of this court that the defendant, defined under the law as artificial and inhuman, be sentenced to serve a term of imprisonment in the Department of Corrections of this Europan colony that lasts the extent of its unnatural life.

> **Judge Hrang: District Eta Court**
> **6.25.2145 CE**

7.7.2145

The prison is separated from the rest of the Europan colony by a long narrow tunnel of ice. The tunnel is not supported by the same atmosphere or life support systems as the main settlement. It does not have breathable air and those traveling must wear a pressurized suit. In order to obtain such a suit, one needs special dispensation from the governor's office. Travel from the main settlement via any tunnel to the surface, to the science outposts, to the drill site and mines of the geological survey team, or to the prison is closely regulated. Normally only guards and prisoners (who will not return the way they came) travel this tunnel.

"Comfortable?" The guard does not even turn his head. The suit makes this difficult, but he can hear Aiya's breathing in his comms as she can hear his.

"Hardly." She is not used to walking in a suit. She rarely leaves her own grid, much less the main settlement of the district.

"You'll get used to it. It's only a little over two kilometers."

In Aiya's district, every place she goes—the commissary, her offices, the doctor—are less than half a kilometer from her own domicile. The Europan settlements are economical in their use of space, if nothing else.

There are small LEDs embedded every meter along the way of the tunnel, so the light is thin, their shadows sharp. She tries to forget that there is a whole ocean below her, less than fifty kilometers away. It is hard to ignore the fact with the stark, alien ice crowded so close.

"I could have requisitioned a shuttle," the guard says, and he leaves his reasoning for not doing so implicit.

"I'm fine." She is used to being underestimated by the military men and women who still make up the majority of the population. The prison, even though it houses civilians, is still managed by the army, so she knows her escort must be soldier first and prison guard second.

She clears her throat. The guard takes it as a cue to initiate conversation.

"Very few ever make parole," he volunteers. "You say you're here with the rehabilitation program? Not sure I see the point of it."

Aiya doesn't have an answer ready. It is a new program, established by the governor in hopes of reincorporating inmates into the workforce. The pool of available labor, after all, is limited here in a way it never was on Earth.

"I volunteered for a similar program in the Americas," she says by way of excuse. "It's a way to get back to feeling normal."

He nods in understanding. "It can wreck you, the transition."

She keeps her eyes down, watching her own step. There are metal grilles set in the ice for grip. She has been here for over a year and she still feels unbalanced. "I'm here to see an incarcerated *robotnik*."

The guard stops and turns to look at her. She can see his eyes, suspicious, through the reflections of the lights on his faceplate. "You're going to try and rehabilitate one of those grunts?"

She nods. Then she shrugs her shoulders.

"I don't understand why we waste resources on them as it is. Why not a hard reboot and send them back to their jobs?" He turns forward again.

"UN resolution. 2139."

The guard shakes his head and picks up the pace. "Don't know why we went to space if we're still tied up in all that policy shit." He mutters this under his breath, but the comms make that meaningless. She does not answer. She tries to catch her breath.

She glances at the monitor on the arm of her suit. It tracks how long they've walked, how far they've come, calories burned, rate of oxygen consumption, amount of oxygen remaining, and a few other stats she is unsure of. The tunnel begins to climb upward. The prison is closer to the irradiated surface of the moon. She can feel sweat on her arms and in the small of her back, and on her forehead where the helmet presses close. There is almost a kilometer left before they reach the prison.

The lights in the tunnel blink rapidly red, then white, then red again. They stay red for a space of thirty seconds and then lapse back to their normal steady white. Aiya pauses, places a hand on the tunnel wall to steady herself. The girder is solid under her hand. The guard does not even stop.

"What was that?" she asks.

"Test of the prison emergency alert system," he answers.

He glances at his monitor. "Nothing to worry about."

The tunnel begins to widen. They pass bays set into the tunnel wall, occupied by shuttles with armored sides and roofs. Other men and women, in suits painted with the prison insignia, cross paths with them. The guard nods to some of them, bobbing his shoulders as well to underscore the gesture.

By the time they reach the prison, the tunnel has opened out into a high, broad man-made cave, like an oversized cathedral. Aiya's legs are sore, and the air in her suit is warm. She only nods when the guard turns around and gives the thumbs up, asking her to confirm that she is ready. She is not sure what to expect. There are a number of geodesic domes that circle the main prison compound. These are where the guards and administrators live with their families. In addition to the domes, there are small pods built to minimum UN standards to house the *robotnici* that work in the prison complex. They are normally hard to distinguish from the humans, but here they wear neon-colored jumpsuits.

"This way," the guard says, and Aiya realizes that she has stopped walking.

The prison itself is large for a Europan structure, overshadowing the domes and pods around it. There is one main entrance, a double set of doors with an airlock. A pair of guards, armed with electric pistols that could depower any suit with life-support functions, wait for the guard escorting Aiya to show his credentials.

"Come on." The guards at the door type paired passwords into the security system and the first door slides up. Her escort gestures for her to follow. She tries to smile at the guards on duty as she passes them, but she is not sure they can really see her face.

"This is your first time at the prison, right?" Once they have passed through the second door, the guard takes off his helmet.

"Yes." She follows his lead and releases the catch at the base of her helmet. The air in the pressurized hallway feels fresh after the extended time spent in her suit. She pushes her hair back from her forehead.

"Just remember. Don't trust any of them. Don't let your guard down. If they're in here, they're desperate."

"So it seems," she answers, remembering the lights blinking in the tunnel.

"I mean it," he says. He looks at her, points a finger very close to her face. "If you're going to be here, you need to understand that."

"I do." She tries to sound sincere.

The guard leads her through the steps necessary to gain access to the prison: signing in with an officer behind a barred window, receiving a temporary ID bracelet with her unique identifiers and medical history that syncs with the watch and computer on her wrist, and waiving her rights to sue if something were to go wrong inside. She reads this last part of the form with extreme prejudice, noting loopholes the authors have not closed.

"I don't have all day here," the guard says, even though it has only been a minute or two.

She smiles at him, her most professional of smiles. "Thank you for your patience, officer." She is not sure of his rank. "If you can take me to the cell of—" She consults the prisoner's file on her watch. "Worker-class, ID 812-3." Her voice grows quiet as she says it, having anticipated an actual name, a pseudonym at least.

"D block, cell 2." The officer behind the window digitally adds the information to her ID bracelet, and her escort nods his head.

The walk is not long. The walls of the passages are constructed in something that looks like corrugated cardboard to Aiya's eyes, though it sounds like metal when she taps on it. Many of the cells that they pass, closed off from the corridor by thick doors with small windows, are dark and empty. In the fourteen years since District Eta, the fifth settlement on Europa, opened to civilian citizens, there have been mercifully few prison sentences passed down by the court. The prison is built to hold many more. *So optimistic*, Aiya thinks.

A sharp right and a set of stairs take them to D block.

It is dark, and the lights are activated by their motion. At the second cell door, the guard stops, takes the glove off his right hand, and presses his thumb to the lock. The door slides back into the wall, almost without noise. Aiya waits a moment, looking into the darkness of the cell. The guard says nothing. She takes a step forward and the lights flicker on inside.

The prisoner is staring at her. Or rather, he is staring at the door, unmoving, and she walks into his line of sight.

"Hello," she stutters, shaken by the way he does not move or blink. "I am Aiya Ritsehrer."

"In or out," the guard says behind her. So she steps in, and the door slides shut behind her. A camera on the ceiling swivels to focus on her. The officer will be watching.

She tries to remember the information passed to her by the district clerk who manages the rehabilitation program. What crime has the prisoner committed? Is he violent? Any lawyer should know better than to waive her rights to sue.

The prisoner has still not talked. He looks, in most respects, like a human. He presents, as far as she can tell, as a man, so she assigns him those pronouns in her head. She is not sure if *robotnici* even identify themselves by gender.

"I am Aiya Ritsehrer," she repeats, "and I am here on behalf of District Eta's Prisoner Rehabilitation Program."

He does not answer. At first.

Pitched camp on elevated ridge one kilometer from geyser Crete. Two days out from nearest intraplanetary shuttle. Rover handled the terrain well. Suits are registering temperatures below-160 C. Radiation strong as expected. Ganymede is in the sky. Prepping for first approach to geyser tomorrow, where there is the highest likelihood we will find alien life.

In the wake of the UN resolution banning the re-programming of those AI which have been in a state of consciousness (hereafter referred to as "alive") longer than six months, the prison system in the Americas has been faced with a new dilemma: the incarceration of AI in unforeseen numbers. Research shows that the rate of recidivism in this population is unexpectedly high as well. In response, rehabilitation programs have been extended to include AI prisoners alongside human ones. This article attempts to show, in part, which aspects of those programs are most usefully applied to this new AI population.

Abstract: VanDerl, M.J., A.P. Carl, L.V. Singh. "AI Recidivism and Rehabilitation Programs in the Americas: A Survey and Analysis," *Journal of New Sociology,* 7.2 (2143)

7.7.2145

When the *robotnik* finally does talk, he speaks first about his job. He does not introduce himself. He does not ask Aiya to explain more fully why she is in his cell. He does not shake her hand or offer to move so that she might also sit on the cot. It does not matter. She does not want to sit near him. He does not blink. She continues to stand just inside the door, and she finds comfort knowing the officer is on the other side.

"Who is replacing me at the drill?" he asks.

Aiya does not know much about his former job. "Do you miss your job?"

He turns his head away from her, and she does not know how to interpret the motion. She tries not to imagine gears or ball bearings, tries not to describe the motion as *swiveling*. It matters, she knows, the words you use. Words can save or damn a person on the stand.

"What is your name?"

The *robotnik* looks at her again. The corners of his mouth lift slightly. "You don't know? That's strange, isn't it? You came here without knowing my name?"

"What do you call yourself?" she asks again.

"The supervisors don't encourage it."

"To have a name other than Worker-class 812-3? Maybe it's not encouraged, but I know there must be some other name."

He still does not blink. She has time to study his face since he does not answer right away. His skin is chipped and mottled. It almost reminds her of that of a damaged porcelain doll, though his skin is much more lifelike than that. It looks as if it might be warm.

"You know? How do you know?" She expects aggression or anger from the question itself, but his voice is level.

———————

"This one will turn your stomach," Ghita said. He took his helmet off as the door closed and locked behind them. The light above the door blinked green to indicate pressure and atmosphere were stable. Only then did Ray follow his example. He removed his suit carefully. There were hooks on the wall from which to hang suits and helmets. Most of the suits already there were marked by the fluorescent white stripes of the mining operations.

The floor below them vibrated from the drills boring into Europa's mantle.

"They haven't shut down the drills?" Ray asked.

Ghita shrugged. He smoothed his hair back with both hands as if he had just doused his face in water. "No need, I guess. The body is out of the way of the primary operations."

————————

"Perhaps I misspoke. I assumed," Aiya answers carefully. "It's a mouthful."

"Aiya Ritsehrer. Isn't that a mouthful?" His eyes are still. She does not know if he can laugh, and she cannot tell if he is mocking her or simply making an observation.

"You can just call me Aiya."

"For those like me, numbers are not difficult names. It seems natural. Why are you here, Aiya?"

The question is expected, but the context throws her off. There is no pause, no intake of breath to signal the change in direction. Her answer feels inadequate, but she provides it anyway.

"As I mentioned when I came in, I'm with the Prisoner Rehabilitation Program." She knows she should say something else. "I can help you access mental health and educational services. If you would like to pursue a degree, or if you would like to set up a work arrangement with the colony, I can help with that too."

He turns his head away again. She wants to laugh, because she is anxious, because her heart is beating so fast.

Still staring at the far wall—where there are no pictures, no calendar, no marks—he says, "How many *robotnici* have completed a degree? Are there books on the psychology of AI?"

"There are precedents." She breathes in deeply, releases slowly.

———————

"Well, let's get this over with." Ray stepped forward to the opaque doors that divided them from the larger facilities beyond.

He stooped so his eyeball could be scanned by the security panel. Both he and Ghita, as military police, had access to enter any structure in the district, so the door slid open almost immediately. The noise level spiked drastically as they moved into the nested chambers of the mine. Each chamber was open to the dome above and could be reached by a central path that intersected them all. The whining sounds of the drills bounced and echoed and filled every corner of the interior. There was a fine dust that looked like snow. It was cold in the chamber.

In the outer chamber where they stood, the walls were carved from natural rock and ice. To their right, that rock and ice was spattered with blood.

———————

"Are you a lawyer?" he asks.

Aiya wonders if his access to the colony's network has

been properly shut down. "Why do you ask?" She tries to hold her hands very still in front of herself.

"You used the word *precedent*. It seems like the type of word a lawyer would use." He stands up, and he moves to the far wall of the cell. He faces her from it, standing very still and upright. "Based on what I've seen. In the shows." He holds his hands in front of himself.

"Well, I am. A lawyer." She does not look back at the door. She does not let her eyes wander.

"Do you really think that work will—" And here he finally pauses, shows some hesitation. "—rehabilitate me?"

She swallows and huffs in her throat, an approximation of a laugh. "Perhaps that does sound a bit odd in your case."

"Do you know what they said I did?" His skin looks unwell, the color so unexpected, like that of a very sick man or a man of metal.

She notes the word *said*. She tries to lock away the memory of how he is standing and what his voice sounds like when he says it.

"Something of it." But she deliberately avoided reading anything about him. She didn't want to enter into the cell with any preconceptions. She thinks now that this was a mistake.

"I killed a man."

———————

"It's there." Ghita pointed. One of the site's supervisors waited near where Ghita indicated. He looked uncomfortable, even from this distance, holding his arms close to his chest, refusing to look at the mound at the base of the wall. He did not talk to them when they drew close, just nodded curtly.

"As far as I can tell—the lab can confirm—head nearly hacked off with the drill bit. Would take some strength." Ghita cleared his throat. There was not much to smell, as cold as this chamber was, but the sight was unsettling enough without it. "Maybe a grunt? That's my best guess at this point."

———————

Aiya cannot help thinking, in the moment of silence when she can hear her own breath grow more frantic, that she knew when she signed on to come to Europa that it would be a society new to her. The colonies drew the best and the worst, those mislabeled or unlabeled. "Criminals go to the colonies," her mother said, sipping her coffee as if she would see her daughter again very soon. "Not for the most part," Aiya answered, keeping her voice calm. "Though there are some work programs." This is how she sparred with her mother, answering an exaggerated claim with its smaller counterpart, the truth. "This isn't the eighteenth century."

"And did you?" It is not the right question to ask. She knows this. Because she does not want to know the answer. She suspects the truth is unpleasant.

"You've already made up your mind," he says. "I have learned there is no point after that."

"How do you know that I've made it up?"

"The way you're standing. The way you're looking at me."

And still he does not blink. He does not look sad or angry. His face is smooth and unchanging. She looks down at her feet, tries to see how she is standing. She is leaning forward on her toes, just a little.

"Look," she says, "I'm just here to help in what way I can." Her face flushes red. She can feel it.

"Something like that." He moves back to the cot and sits down. She feels that she has failed some test. "Why rehabilitate a killer? Do they want me back at the survey site? You never answered my question."

———

Ray knelt down next to the body and gently rolled it onto its back from its initial position, a fetal curl. A careful map-

ping of the body's position and the surrounding area had already been recorded by the small droid that rolled now between their feet and up the wall, taking note of everything they did for later 3D re-experience as necessary.

As the body fell onto its back, the head lolled dangerously off the neck, the vertebrae partially severed by the force of the attack. The edges of the wound, where the throat split wide, were jagged and uneven. Ray glanced at the drill bit that lay abandoned a short ways off, blood crusted on the flute. He reached into the wound, probing the vertebrae with two fingers.

"Hey," Ghita scolded him, "Coroner still needs to get in there."

There was no electric shock, no metal rod or cabling in the vertebrae. "Just confirming he's human."

Aiya relaxes her stance, leans back against the door and likes the feel of it close. "I'm sorry I don't know anything about your job."

"Has anyone asked after me? Who sent you?"

"Like I said, I came as part of the program."

"No one said *go and look after 812-3*?" And the number does sound more natural, more like a name the way he says it. "They didn't say *I miss him and I worry about him alone*."

She shifts uneasily, because this does not sound like anything he has said before. The tone of his voice, the clumsy words, remind her unexpectedly of a child.

"I'm sorry. I'm not sure what you're asking."

He nods his head slowly. "No, of course not. It doesn't matter."

He drew his hand back, wiped it clean on the close-fitting leggings he had worn under his suit. He made a mental note to dispose of the leggings when he returned home.

"The murderer, though." Ghita shook his head. "Imagine doing that with a drill bit."

A layer of dust had settled on the corpse, riming the features of the face—down to the hairs of the eyebrows and eyelashes—with granules of ice and rock.

"The drill bit," the supervisor broke in, clearing his throat many times as he spoke, "belongs to our smaller machines, intended for detail work or probing. They are generally handheld, and many are operated by our robotnici."

"Like I said." Ghita punctuated his remark.

"Why, though?" Ray asked.

"Why do they do anything?"

"Programming." Ray looked down at the victim's face. He seemed relatively young, dark hair cut short to the head. He

wore a silicon wedding ring on his left hand. "That's why it doesn't make any sense."

Ghita shook his head. "I've seen enough in prison not to question it."

"Really? That's the same thing that makes me keep asking questions." Ray looked at the supervisor. "No security camera?"

"Normally, yes." The supervisor looked at the ground. "But we had reports of corporate espionage, a hack on our feeds, so we went black for a number of hours last night. In order to update our systems."

The officer bangs on the door. Aiya leaps back from it and she is standing close to the *robotnik*.

"I need to go soon. In a few minutes," she explains. He does not look up or seem to care. "Is there something I can set up for you? I'll visit again."

"Please don't visit again," he says. His voice is flat.

"It's all part of the program," she answers. "I'll bring you some books? Or show you a college curriculum?"

"Yes." He does not say which one he is assenting to.

"Time," the officer shouts from the other side. He is unlocking the door. She can hear the mechanisms shifting and tumbling.

"Are you alright?" she asks, instinctively. She does not know if she wants to hear the answer.

"Fine."

She lifts her hand in a half-hearted way as if to wave goodbye and stumbles out of the cell when the officer opens it. She smooths her shirt and does not look as the officer closes the door again. She hears the hiss of the door's seal.

"Have fun?" her escort asks.

She wants to tell him to shut up, but she is facing a long walk back to the main colony with him. She shakes her head. "You warned me."

"Didn't I?" And he tucks his gun back in his belt.

"I hope the updates were worth it." Ghita watched Ray as *he stepped back from the corpse. The supervisor shrugged his shoulders.*

"We'll need to speak to everyone who works here. How many you have here? Fifty?" Ray opened a note on his watch and waited for the supervisor to answer.

"Ten or eleven trained specialists. Two scientists for now. And thirty-five grunts. They stay on the premises at all times. Housing opposite the drills." The supervisor waved in that direction. "But I can't think of a single one

who would do something like this."

"Do you know their names? Their IDs?" Ray asked.

The supervisor laughed, nervously, under his breath. "Off the top of my head? Of course not."

"Then how well do you really know them?"

"I know the type."

Ray looked at the corpse. "With all due respect, I think we might need to redefine the type."

When Aiya reports the results of her prison visit, the district clerk gives her access to a folder of video files in the court's network—primarily because the same footage was accessible to a wider audience at the time of 812-3's conviction.

Later, after her partner goes to bed, she watches the files. They contain the body cam footage of the military police at the crime scene. She watches them as they enter the survey site, as they examine the body, hacked cruelly open, and as they talk with the supervisor on duty. She sits very still as she watches and her mouth is dry. She knocks over her glass of water when she reaches for it as the footage ends. She lets it drip from the table to the tiled floor. She turns off the screen of her tablet.

The lights in the domicile are dim to indicate that it

is night, as if the darkness of Earth were pressing against the narrow windows. She presses her hands against her eyes, and tries to pretend the tears are not there, that her cheeks are not wet.

CAMP JOURNAL, 8.10.2145
@ CRETE, GEYSER

Approached geyser on foot. Inactive today. Collected samples of salt residue, cores. At geyser, ridges impede view to the horizon. Joints are stiff from cold and salt.

(b) Murder is the unlawful killing of a human being with malice aforethought. Every murder perpetuated by an artificial intelligence, whether it be by physical, digital, or manipulative means; or committed by a human at the behest, threat, or manipulation of an artificial intelligence, is murder in the first degree with inhuman intent.

17 Americas Code § 1112

7.8.2145

Aiya wakes up late and she feels groggy as if she drank too much the night before. She can hear Peri in the kitchen. Their stove amounts to nothing more than a camp stove, but she assumes that Peri is making powdered eggs, as she has insisted on doing most mornings since they arrived at the colony. She puts her head in her hands and sits for a moment with the pain at her temples.

The bot, which cleans the floors, recycles the waste, and monitors their energy use, moves into her room, the brushes in its undercarriage whispering against the floor. "Sorry, sorry," it repeats as it bumps against her feet. It stands almost to her calf, a shiny dome with a monitor in lieu of a face and a row of lights on its crown. Its voice is tinny.

"No problem," she says. She puts a finger over her lips afterward and feels foolish for answering.

"Are you talking to me?" Peri shouts to her from the kitchen.

Aiya does not answer. She stands up and goes to the mirror on the wall and the shelf underneath that serves as a nightstand. She combs out her hair and braids it tight. She curls it into a bun at the nape of her neck.

"Did you say something?" Peri appears in the doorway. She is still in her nightgown.

"No. I was just talking to the bot."

"The bot?" Peri raises her eyebrow. She holds a plate of eggs in her hand. They smell like onions and garlic. "There are more in the pan if you want any," she says when she notices Aiya's glance.

Aiya shakes her head. Peri takes a deep breath, indicating that she does not want to ask any more questions but will anyway. Their domestic partnership is platonic, arranged in accordance with Europan regulations that all civilian settlers be accompanied by a partner, romantic or otherwise. Both single at the time they applied for transfer, Aiya and Peri were assigned to each other by a battery of tests. The tests had been largely accurate, but not perfect.

"Is this something to do with your visit to the prison yesterday?"

"What do you mean?"

"You look like shit. You're not eating."

"Maybe I don't want eggs again."

Peri mutters something under her breath about superfoods, and Aiya sets down the comb and stares in the mirror—which is small, much like the room and much like the domicile. She touches a finger to her cheek and pokes the skin.

"What are you doing?"

"Hm?" Aiya looks at Peri, looks at the way that her shoulders link to her arms, her head to her neck.

"What are you doing?" Peri is irritated now. She forks a mouthful of egg.

"Didn't we name the bot at one time?"

"I don't know. Like a pet? I think we nicknamed it Rosie when we first settled in. After the Jetsons."

The bot beeps quietly, under its breath if it had any. Aiya looks at it.

"What happened yesterday?" Peri walks toward the kitchen but her voice drifts back. "What were you watching last night?"

Aiya tells her about 812-3 and the murder. It is easier to do when she is not in the same room. Peri is quiet when Aiya finishes talking. Aiya wonders if she has wandered out of hearing. She leaves her own room and pokes her head into the kitchen. Peri scrapes her plate into the disposal, then sprays it with fast-drying detergent, wipes it down with a towel. The bot tracks their water consumption.

"Is there any coffee?"

Peri nods toward the carafe. Aiya pours herself some.

"I don't think it's a good idea," Peri finally says.

Aiya sips. "What isn't?"

"Working with that thing."

She sets down the coffee. It is almost too hot anyway. "He says he didn't do it."

"It said that?"

"Sort of."

Peri laughs. Not in a happy way. "It's not really a matter of what it says anyway, is it? There are memory files."

"By law—" Aiya begins.

"By law!" Scorn and mockery in her voice.

"By law, we can no longer access an AI's files without consent."

"That doesn't make any sense." Peri scraped the remainder of the eggs into the disposal. Her arm moves in quick, fierce jerks. "We make them. We manufacture them. We should control them. We can't have it both ways. Give them human rights and still treat them like slaves."

"So better we strip the rights?"

Peri's back trembles. She is angry or she is crying. Or both. "Either they're machines or we're monsters."

"Well, the latter's a given." It's the type of thing Aiya says to be funny.

Peri turns back to the sink and scrubs clean the pan. Her face is flushed but not wet. "If you're joking about it, I think that tells you what you need to know. You shouldn't be doing this."

"What am I doing? Giving a grunt some books? Talking philosophy with him?"

"Him?"

Aiya leans back against the counter. She stands close by Peri. "It's easier to say, isn't it?"

"It says a lot."

Aiya puts her hand on Peri's arm. "You're too upset about this." And she shoves away the memory of the night before. She notices how warm Peri's skin is.

"No such thing," Peri says. "You're as upset as you need to be. In any moment."

Aiya does not agree but she remains quiet. Peri sighs, and she relaxes. She dries her hands. "I'm sorry. But if something happens to you, I don't have anyone else. I can't just hop the next ship back to Earth."

"What could happen? I'm a former public defender working as a property lawyer. In what might as well be a small town for all the gossip."

"It killed someone and I don't trust it."

"I never said I did." Aiya's voice is quiet. "Hey, don't worry about it. I'm sorry I even brought it up."

"Sure." But the way you say something matters, and Aiya does not believe Peri. "I'm going to get dressed and see if they have anything new in at the commissary."

She shuffles out of the kitchen. Aiya tries her coffee again and finds it now too cool. She pours it out in the sink. For a moment, it stains the white surface. There is a small beep behind her. A red number flashes on the droid's monitor as it registers the waste.

"It's alright, Rosie," she says.

CAMP JOURNAL, 8.11.2145
@ CRETE, GEYSER

While at rest, heard creaking sounds like glaciers at sea.
Earthquakes and disruptions kept us inside today. Impossible to use the scientific equipment.

We cannot—we will not—abide this sort of vigilante justice which has no regard for due process. I understand, I am human, I understand the urge to seek out your own justice when looking into the eyes of one of them. But we must rise above our first instincts and prove ourselves human even when facing the inhuman.

Governor Paolo Martine: District Eta
7.21.2145 CE

7.14.2145

"I want to appeal." 812-3 hardly waits for her to sit down before he speaks. He taps a finger to his thigh on every word, as if he has rehearsed the request.

"I'm sorry." She is not sure what she is apologizing for. She is caught off guard. She sets down her bag and feels the weight of the books she has brought settling on the floor. The district won't let her bring a tablet to the prisoner, nor would he have access to the network any longer. It is hard to find actual books in the colony. There is an ex-military man—he now works for the drill site—who collects and sells odds and ends that remind the settlers of Earth. She thumbed through his small collection of paperback books before trekking to the prison.

She did not request an escort from the main colony. To anyone who stopped her, she flashed the pass provided by the district clerk, taped to the outer arm of her suit. When she arrived at the prison entrance, she was almost sure that one of the guards flashed a derogatory signal to his partner as she turned her back on them. The doors closed and the seal popped. The oxygen levels rose and she unlatched her helmet. She took a large breath and coughed. She measured her pulse at her wrist. And then she was led to the prisoner's cell.

Now he stares at her, unblinking.

"An appeal," he repeats.

She swallows, tries to relax in the chair that has been provided for her this time.

"I'm sorry—is this because I said I was a lawyer? That's not why I'm here."

"I know it is not why you came. But it is the only thing I want from you."

She looks at the bag of books and sighs. She tries a different tack. "There are no appellate courts on Europa." It is, strictly speaking, true. The transition from military to civilian courts has been difficult on Europa. Very little of the bureaucracy and infrastructure was prepared to handle the influx of civilian settlers.

"I have rights," he says. She nods, indicating that she is listening. "If I am tried in the court of law, I can make an appeal within thirty days."

"On what grounds?" She realizes she has already made up the gridwork in her head, the one on which she keeps mental notes for her cases. In her past experience, she was never sure what detail might be of use, and certain mnemonics were useful for catching things she didn't write down.

"What grounds?"

"On what grounds do you want to make the appeal? Did your lawyer make a mistake? Evidence tampering? Jury? Why do you think you deserve an appeal?"

"I didn't do it."

"Didn't do what?" She needs to hear the words.

He sits very still, very stiff, on the edge of the cot. His jumpsuit almost looks as if it has been pressed. It bends at right angles on his body. He looks at her, his eyes wide. He blinks, just as she is wondering whether he blinks.

"I didn't murder Derrien Cho."

She has not heard the victim's name yet. Neither of the police in the footage she watched mentioned it.

"Did you know him?" She moves forward in her own chair.

"Does it matter?" He places a hand over his eyes, for less than ten seconds. Then he returns his hand to his lap.

"More likely to murder someone you know than otherwise."

"I didn't kill him. That is what I said."

"I heard you."

They sit in silence for a moment. Then she bends over and lifts up her bag. "I brought some books in case you might be bored." She isn't sure if *robotnici* can be bored.

"I don't want books. I want you to submit an appeal on my behalf."

"There is nowhere to submit one to." This seems like the easier answer.

"You say there are no appellate courts on Europa. There are on Earth. In the Americas."

"Yes."

He is waiting for her to say more. He bends his head forward an inch. "There must be some contingency in place."

"Our district is one of five on Europa, two of which are American. In this district, the majority of the citizens are military, and they handle their affairs internally, via courts based on Earth. Only fourteen years of civilian settlement. Let's say, then, roughly four thousand people. Four thousand civilians. Of those, one is a qualified judge. The cases brought to him are extreme ones." She does not mention 812-3's own case. "Open and shut cases. I don't even know what plan is in place if anyone were to request an appeal."

"Four thousand civilians," he repeats. "And 3,702 *robotnici*. And one of them is requesting an appeal."

"Do you know how many *robotnici* are held here?"

He does not pause. "Four. Including myself."

"Yeah, so you're a strange case already."

"It is my right."

"Debatable." She says it flippantly.

"Pursuant to the UN resolution, under the second amendment of the American Articles—"

She interrupts him. "I know the law." He cuts off abruptly, like a stopped audio file. "Nonetheless, some might debate it."

"Then set a precedent," he answers. He emphasizes the word *precedent* and Aiya realizes he is deliberately alluding to their first visit. The transparency of his persuasive technique makes her uneasy. "Submit an appeal. To wherever you have to."

"It's not just a technical question."

"What kind of question is it?"

"It's a question of whether I want to."

He nods his head, presses his lips close as if he is thinking of his next words carefully. "What would convince you?"

She told Peri, when they first met, why she was leaving her job and her country and her planet. They were reviewing their lists of likes and dislikes, testing whether a partnership was tenable. They were drinking filtered water, flavored with artificial lemon. *"I don't like it," she said. "I defend the innocent. I defend the guilty. I defend the mediocre and the monstrosities between. I am tired of human confidences."* Peri had laughed, and now, from a distance, Aiya wonders if she knew how sincerely she meant it.

"Probably nothing you can say," she answers 812-3. "I'm here with the rehabilitation program. I'm not here to serve as your lawyer."

"But if I am innocent, how can I be rehabilitated?"

"It's not about how you came in, but how you leave. Prison is prison."

He moves suddenly toward her, standing up. He is tall, and his head blocks part of the light from the strips in the wall. "You have to help me."

His words are desperate, but his face is calm, his shoulders relaxed.

"Guard." She looks toward the camera. "Open the door." She stands up and moves behind her chair, putting it between them.

"I won't hurt you," he says. But she looks at his hands. They are curled into fists.

The door slides open.

"Back against the wall," the guard barks. He holds a stun gun in his hand.

812-3 glances from it to the guard's face. He looks again at Aiya. "Isn't it your job?"

The gun makes a popping noise, like that of a toy, when it fires. A small pellet burrows into the AI's shoulder and he spasms. He steps backward, trips, and collapses against the wall. His limbs jerk as she snatches up her bag and steps out of the cell.

"I don't ask twice," the guard says to 812-3, and he closes the door. The two of them stand alone in the hallway.

When she prepares to leave the prison, she double-checks that her helmet is securely fastened. Her fingers are trembling and hard to use in the large gloves. The door opens and she sees the dome of rock and ice, the tunnel beyond. The geodesic dome shines whiter than the ice in the lights. The lights are affixed to tall poles, like those that ran alongside highways back home. And she feels isolated like she did when she stepped out of her car at night and stood by the highway and watched the dotted yellow lines of the road fading into the darkness ahead of her, the road infinite and then gone. The heat, the smothering silence, of a night in summer.

CAMP JOURNAL, 8.12.2145
@ CRETE, GEYSER

Concern about contamination of the samples in the wake of the quakes.

a glance of light on

metal bright

sight like love at first

haiku

Scribal-class, ID 742-12

7.15.2145

Aiya stands in the chamber outside the main drilling operations. The supervisor, someone named Daviis, hovers
near her.

"Who gave you access?" he asks again, as if he hopes
to trip her up in a lie.

The drills are operating at full capacity and the ground
beneath her trembles, making her wonder if the overall
structure is safe. She glances up at the dome of ice that
soars above the inner chamber walls. Small particles of
ice fall like snowflakes. She has not bothered to remove

most of her suit, but her gloves and helmet are in the air-lock. She waddles as she walks. The droid rolls forward and back near her feet, as if impatient to begin.

"District Eta captain." Not that the permission was easily granted. She used what little pull she had with the district clerk to gain the captain's ear. He did not understand at first why she wanted to visit the mines.

"Not our VP then?"

She looks at him. "I assume he was consulted. Look, I won't be here long. Just enough to run the scene."

He tucks his hands into the pockets of his tailored jumpsuit. "Hurry, please."

She bends down and taps the droid as if petting a small dog. It lurches forward on its wheels. It moves in a series of circles, rapidly expanding its route into larger ellipses. As it maneuvers, the droid builds a virtual re-creation of the same murder scene she had viewed in the video footage a week before, overlaid on the rock and ice of the chamber floor and walls. The mesh of light and color makes the image unsettlingly real.

Aiya bends into the light, the laser gridwork dancing in her eyes and on her skin. She tries to lay a hand on the victim's chest, but it is unsubstantial. She can see the neck bent at an awkward angle, the blood and viscera, the tattered skin.

"Why do you want to look at this?" Daviis's voice is

rough in his throat.

"With a drill bit?" She cranes her neck to look at him.

"Brutal." He doesn't exactly answer the question.

"Was his partner compensated?" She points at the wedding ring on the corpse's left hand.

Daviis bobs his head. "Standard life insurance policy."

"Isn't that the first question they always ask?" She imagines that she looks like an investigator in a crime drama, hunched close to Cho's body.

"Yes." The supervisor is not amused. His tone reminds her of the reality of the situation.

"I'm sorry that I inconvenienced you," she says quietly. She stands up and signals the droid. The virtual re-creation blinks and disappears. As she stretches her back, she glances toward the door of the next chamber. Someone is watching them. The person stands stiffly, her arms hanging unnaturally still at her sides. The supervisor follows Aiya's glance. He snaps his finger and gestures angrily at the worker. The grunt turns on her heel and retreats into the mine.

"Are they upset about the murder?"

Daviis opens his mouth but takes a moment to answer. "I'm not sure. They haven't said anything to me. Work hasn't suffered. And it's been almost a year since they found the body. I doubt they even have those sort of reflexive capabilities."

Aiya remembers 812-3's first question to her. "Who is replacing him? The one found guilty."

Daviis shrugs. "Everyone and no one. Work just gets shifted a bit. They can handle more than they're doing now."

"They have a breaking point too, don't they?"

"Haven't found it yet." Daviis crosses his arms. "Are we done here?"

She wants to contradict, wants to order the droid to pull back up the image of the victim, of the blood splattered on the wall and floor.

"Yeah. Thank you." She shakes his hand. His palm is sweaty. He leads her to the airlock door and watches as she goes in. She puts on her helmet and gloves and lifts her hand to say goodbye. He doesn't move. The door to the inner chamber slides shut and she turns to face the outside door. She waits for the pressure to equalize, signaled by a small green light at the northeast corner of the door.

The light blinks green.

"Why? Give me a good reason, Ms. Ritsehrer." The captain looked at her from across his desk. The clerk shrugged her shoulders when Aiya glanced at her for help.

"He's asked me to submit an appeal. I need to see the crime for myself."

"It's simpler than you're making it." He crossed his hands at the waist, holding the wrist of one in the other. "You just say no. There's no precedent here anyway. No court ready to handle it. And, if you need reminding, calling it 'he' doesn't make it human."

"Not trying to make it human, sir. Just due diligence. Before I say no."

"But you're saying no? I'll give you access if it helps you to the right answer."

She nodded and swallowed down any doubt.

The light blinks again, insistent.

Injury at the collection site, at Crete's mouth, with one of the drills. I carried the technician back to the camp.

e) Termination is the unlawful reprogramming or rebooting of an artificial intelligence deemed sentient with malice aforethought. Every termination perpetrated by a human or artificial intelligence, whether it be by physical, digital, or manipulative means, is murder in the third degree.

17 Americas Code § 1113

7.16.2145

Peri brings lunch to the office on days when Aiya will be working late. Aiya is not planning on working late today, though, so she is surprised when Peri comes in. She is holding two bento boxes. She takes her time assembling the lunch on the table. Aiya moves her tablet and notes out of the way and watches her because she is very quiet. Rice travels well, so it is a popular food on Europa. Peri has made rice and tofu, easy and kosher for Aiya's sake. She offers Aiya utensils and sits down.

Outside the window, the artificial lights are bright, imitating noon.

"I'll be home normal time today," Aiya finally says, sitting across from Peri.

"I wasn't sure," Peri answers. She is taking small bites, hardly eating.

"Something you need to say?" Aiya pushes her box toward the center of the table. She looks at Peri's face, dark with concern, and feels guilt over her abruptness. "Sorry." She struggles for a different question. "Did you finish the design for the new domiciles?" Peri is an architect, trained to design structures for non-Earth environments.

"You know I'm not here to talk about that."

Aiya shuts her mouth. She stares at the table and waits for Peri to say what she wants to say.

"Sometimes I forget how small this district is. Like you said before, small town. You think, in outer space, everything will be far away and distant, and you forget how close other people are."

Aiya nods her head. "Like being on the ship."

"Like an extension of that, yeah." They shared a cabin on the *A.S.N. Hippolyta* in preparation for their living arrangements on Europa, and the living quarters felt like nothing so much as a stuffy apartment complex.

"We're friends, aren't we?" She speaks with her eyes turned down. "I mean, we're in contractual obligation to each other. But aren't we friends?"

Aiya reaches for her hand but she moves it. "Of course, Peri. Why are you so upset?" She hasn't been herself since they talked over eggs. Aiya thinks she knows why, but she refuses to make her argument for her. "More than friends."

Peri smiles a little. She finally raises her head. "If that's the case, I hope you'll listen to me. Really listen."

"Do I not listen to you?"

Peri waves the question aside and bends forward over the table.

"It's a small place, Aiya. Everyone knows that you keep going back to the prison. That you visited the drill site."

"Meaning?"

"People remember the murder. They remember the footage. It wasn't that long ago. Maybe a year."

Aiya leans back in her chair. "I know the case. I don't need the dates recited to me."

"Yeah, you know it too well. You need to drop it. I thought we talked about this."

"I know what you said. You think he's dangerous."

"As did the court. And the judge. It's in prison for a reason. You're going to make enemies if you try to change that." She takes a deep breath, and tries to catch Aiya's eyes. "Think about the opportunity here. A place with so little crime. Why focus on the anomaly? Why focus on the bad things?"

Aiya stands up from the table and she moves back toward her desk. Her office is small, and the furniture takes up the entirety of it. She feels crowded. Absently, she flips through her notes. They outline the easiest way to transfer public property to private hands as District Eta's civilian population grows.

"I came here because I was tired of all that, yeah."

"Then stop it." Peri spreads her arms out wide as if she is offering the world.

"But it's here too. It comes with us. It's not like murder and crime are in the soil of a place."

Peri is quiet for a second as if she is seriously considering that answer. When she speaks, Aiya can tell she hasn't changed her mind.

"But you don't have to be the one to deal with it. It's been dealt with. The grunt is in prison."

"He asked me."

"Asked you what?"

"Asked me to submit an appeal. He says he's not guilty."

Peri swears and shoves her chair back. "You aren't thinking of helping it?"

"That's why I went to the drill site."

"Because you're really thinking of representing it?" Her voice is very quiet now.

"I'm thinking of it."

"Why?"

The question lingers in the room for a moment. Aiya becomes aware of the recycled air. She takes deliberate breaths.

"You hate him, Peri." The words come reluctantly at first, but then they must be said and they come out fast and panicky. "The prison guards hate him. His work supervisor hates him. The captain of the police."

"That's not a reason." She grits her teeth.

"I don't even know if I believe him. Maybe he did do it."

Peri nods. She gestures wordlessly, emphatically.

"But you can't tell me anyone on this planet constitutes a fair jury for him. You can't tell me that's not grounds for appeal. *A jury of your peers.* Or a jury that hasn't already condemned you. That's the least a defendant can ask for. And if we plan to imprison *robotnici,* then we must be prepared to follow the law in every other point as well."

Peri shakes her head. She looks at the ceiling and then at the table. She stacks the bento boxes. Neither of them has eaten much.

"Are you ready for the riots?" she asks. She tucks the boxes into her satchel.

"It doesn't have to be that way."

"You're the one talking about human nature." She slings the satchel over her shoulder. "That why I was hoping you would listen to me. What you decide to do will impact both of us, Aiya. When they come after you, they'll come after me."

"You're hyperbolizing." Aiya's throat feels tight. "No one is going to come after us."

Peri shrugs. She does not seem convinced. "I hope not." She opens the door, and Aiya can hear the noise of the street outside—the people lined up outside the commissary across the way, the buzz of the lightweight shuttles. It is colder outside than inside. It is harder to regulate the temperature within the open arc of the dome that shelters the district.

"I'll see you at home," Aiya says.

Peri does not answer and the door slides shut behind her. Aiya sweeps her arm across her desk in anger, knocking her tablet, notes, and comms system onto the floor. She slumps into her chair and rests her forehead on the clear desk. She listens to her own breathing, to the voices that rise louder than others from outside. Someone is protesting the price of pickled cod and eggs.

"We can never get away," she mutters. She closes her eyes.

CAMP JOURNAL, 8.14.2145
@ CRETE, GEYSER

Xi found microorganisms, like those hypothesized, in the collected samples. Doctors celebrated.

Thus, I wholeheartedly recommend Aiya Rit-sehrer to the offices of the Court in District Eta. She is, above all, a lawyer dedicated to pars-ing the nuances of the law in unusual circum-stances. And, quite frankly, she could use a challenge.

Letter of Recommendation
Reid K. Barcley, J.D.

7.17.2145

There is an earthquake the next day when Aiya visits the prison and informs 812-3 of her decision. It is not an un-usual occurrence and it is not particularly violent, but it makes it hard for her to keep her footing in the tunnels, bal-ancing in the oversized suit. She has petitioned for perma-nent access to the prisons, so her new ID bracelet is bright green. The guards admit her with quiet, angry grimaces.

The route to the cell is familiar to her.

"Your funeral," the guard on the door says as she approaches. She wonders if this means he will not help her if the *robotnik* attacks her.

"Not quite yet," she answers, trying to keep her voice light.

812-3 looks up when she enters the cell. She might call his expression surprise if he were anything other than what he is.

"You came back?" he asks.

"Yes." And she doubts for a second. She is frightened again. She asks herself why she is here. "I will serve as your attorney. And we'll submit your appeal."

He looks at her, and he is so still that she thinks he might be frozen. He blinks. She notices that he blinks. He shakes his head.

"I did not think you would say yes."

"Why did you ask?"

"What other choice did I have?"

She nods. "People will be angry."

"They're not my concern."

"They are. Because where do you go afterward? If the judge orders a new trial, if you're released from prison, if you win—where do you go? Europa is not so big."

He looks down at his hands and weaves his fingers together. His nails are perfectly symmetrical.

"My restrictions are not yours. I could go wherever I want. For me, this colony is not the extent of Europa."

———————

"All of Europa is buzzing with this news." The journalist leans in close, or there is the appearance of it via their satellite connection. She is actually on the space station orbiting Europa, so the delay in communication is almost nonexistent. Aiya leans back instinctively. She wonders if the journalist has ever set foot on Europa.

"Well, District Eta is, at least." Aiya tries to remember the smiles, the facial gestures she practiced so long in the court-room.

"Tell me, explain for our American audience, what is happening with this appeal? On what grounds are you appealing 812-3's conviction?"

"It's pretty simple, Mia. We have, in the Americas, the concept of a jury of your peers. Established in the days of the United States, still a guiding principle now. Rather, I should clarify, not just a guiding principle but a legal necessity."

The journalist waves her hand, gesturing that she is about to cut in. Aiya is tempted to keep going and forestall the inevitable question.

———————

"Who are my peers?" 812-3 leans back on the cot.

"You tell me. Would you consider me your peer?"

She sees him smile for the first time. It looks unnatural to her eyes.

"*You tell me*," he mimics her. "That's exactly what I can't do. Whether I consider you my peer is hardly the question. It's the other way round."

She takes a breath. "You're right. For this cell. When you're talking to me. But that's not your answer out there." She points to the cell door.

He tilts his head to one side. "What is my answer out there?"

———————

"Are you saying . . ." Mia pauses for emphasis. "Are you saying that an AI being tried in court requires a jury of AI?"

Aiya shifts in her seat. She tugs on her blazer. "That is the basis of our appeal. Otherwise, 812-3 faces—as we have seen once before—discrimination. He was convicted before he ever entered the courtroom. If not AI, a more careful selection process to ensure a fair jury that has not prejudged my client."

———————

"A jury of your peers. A jury of other *robotnici,* maybe."

"Implicit, a human is not my equal. Rephrase, I am not equal with a human."

"I want to help you," she says, unable to come up with any better response. "And to do so, I can't be idealistic. We need to argue that the jury selection process was not rigorous enough. That you faced a highly biased jury. If granted a new trial, we seek a jury of unbiased people, AI if possible."

"And where can we find these unbiased humans?"

"I don't know. We'll take it one step at a time. Appeal first."

———————

"I've submitted our appeal to the First Circuit Court in the Americas. As you know, Mia, we do not have any appellate courts instituted on Europa. And I primarily wanted to speak with you today to emphasize to whoever might be listening: a right to an appeal is a constitutional one. That there is no appellate court on Europa is no reason that my client should not have his appeal considered. I urge the First Circuit Court to take this, to take the constitutional rights of our citizens, under advisement."

Mia smiles and nods, her teeth white. "Some would say that the amendment that outlines the rights of AI does not grant full citizenship."

Aiya can feel the sweat behind her ears and on the back of her neck. Her jaws ache where she clenches her teeth.

"It's been a while since I took a class in constitutional law, but if memory serves me right, that's not a question we have to—we can—answer on air."

Mia laughs, and Aiya shifts in her chair again. As Mia thanks Aiya for joining her, Aiya can hear the music of the program rising in volume. She nods and thanks Mia in turn. As their connection goes dead, she hears Mia turn to her producer and say, "Bitch."

She yanks the earpiece out.

———————

"I suppose I should thank you." 812-3's voice raises as in a question.

Aiya lowers her head, shaking it in the negative. "I'm not asking for that."

"Humans don't ask for most things. They still expect them."

She looks at him. "You're always full of observations." She tucks her tablet and her stylus into her bag.

"I have a lot of time on my hands." He glances around

the cell. She almost expects to see tallies or words scratched into the corrugated metal walls. They are bare. She wonders what he sees, whether the computer that is his brain overlays these walls with information she cannot touch or understand.

"So you do not think I killed Derrien Cho?" She does not expect the question, though she should have. 812-3 does not let things go lightly. But she has refused to face the question since she made up her mind.

"I don't know." She does not even know if this answer is true. She is afraid that it is not true, that she thinks 812-3 is guilty.

"Then why are you here?" The words are sharp and remind her of metal. But she often thinks of metal, of wire, of ceramic when she thinks of her client.

"Because I was told not to be here. Not to help you. Many times. And it provided the grounds for your appeal. And right now, that is grounds for me to be here."

He tucks his tongue into his cheek. He turns his eyes to the floor. "I am not guilty," he says again. Each word clear and succinct.

"Right now," she repeats, "we must get you a new trial, so you can demonstrate that."

He runs his hands through his hair. His hair is almost silver, almost translucent. She takes a step forward and places a hand tentatively on his shoulder.

An aftershock from the earthquake rumbles under their feet, as if the moon is an uneasy giant turning in its sleep. She grips his shoulder tighter to steady herself. It feels like muscle and skin under his thin jumpsuit.

"Then do what you can, Aiya Ritsehrer."

Geologist raised questions about core samples. Mobile lab thoroughly cleaned. Suits inspected for contaminants that could be carried into collection sites.

Sponsors: The Americas, Europe, United India, Korean Territories
Signatories: Baltic States, Iranian Protectorate
Topic: Humanity of Artificial Intelligence

The General Assembly,

Urging member nation-states to remember the commonalities between all intelligences, natural or artificial, in light of recent worldwide demonstrations following the execution of Worker-class, ID 17-1, more familiarly known as Bekka,

Recommending that all sponsors, signatories, and members amend their law codes to reflect this commonality, and make unlawful the termination of any artificial intelligence without due process . . .

Resolution 59/3.5
United Nations

7.20.2145

"Looks like your client got into a bit of trouble." The captain draws his words out. He watches her face closely.

Aiya nods at the clerk, thanking her for the cup of water as she sits across the desk from the captain. The clerk ducks out, closing the door behind her.

"That's what your message said." She refuses to look concerned. She crosses her legs. "Are you going to tell me what happened?"

He leans back in his chair and points a remote at the large monitor set into the wall. Four disparate images, feeds from separate surveillance points, merge into one. Aiya recognizes the prison by its corrugated walls and its bleak lighting.

"I wouldn't be so impolitic as to suggest that you might have a delicate constitution—"

"Please just play the video, captain."

He shifts in his seat, his shoulders stiffening. Then he inputs a time stamp. The video glitches as it finds its place and then unfolds. She notices 812-3 first because he is standing alone in a relatively large indoor gymnasium, the Europan version of the prison yard. He stands still, his arms hanging loose at his side, his spine straight. The dark jumpsuit washes him out and increases the effect of his porcelain-doll complexion. As other prisoners trickle into the space, Aiya feels a sense of isolation on 812-3's behalf, one she is sure he does not feel for himself.

"You feel bad for it." The captain's voice breaks in, disbelieving. "Well, keep watching."

She does not look at him or bother to come up with a reply. She keeps her eyes fixed on the screen.

There are not many prisoners once actually counted, but they create an effect of crowd and mass in the way that they circulate at one end of the gymnasium. It is clear that 812-3 is the only *robotnik* present in the room. He knows it. Aiya thinks that he is wary. He takes careful steps, slow steps. He moves in a back-and-forth pattern as if he wishes to look busy and preoccupied though he has no clear aim. Her body grows tense. She realizes that she is leaning forward in her seat and that the captain is watching her closely.

When it happens, it happens quickly.

A knot of prisoners, primarily men, separates from the general crowd. They wear the sleeves of their jumpsuits rolled up to their elbows. One of them—and she thinks it strange to notice it in the dread of the moment—has a sleeve of tattoos, so dark ink crawls over the sun- and cold-burned skin. This prisoner hangs to the back of the group. A lanky woman leads the group. Her hair is shorn close to her head, and she walks with a languid step as if she is used to maneuvering in a suit.

There is no audio in the video, but Aiya places a finger behind her ear anyway, instinctively, as if she might amplify the prisoners' voices.

The knot of prisoners approaches 812-3 and he stops moving. He turns to face them, setting his shoulders and his stance in preparation for conflict. He stands slightly hunched. The woman says something to him. She steps close, so that her body is uncomfortably near that of 812-3. She places a hand on his shoulder. It is not a schoolyard shove or cheap taunt. What she says next is spoken quietly. The men behind her strive to hear her. They are leaning forward in anticipation. 812-3 pulls his head back, his neck moving unnaturally.

Aiya squeezes her fist against her knee.

The man with the tattoo swings his arm up unexpectedly. There is something small and glinting grasped in his hand. In reaction, 812-3 leans back, almost falling onto his outstretched arm. The handmade weapon tears the jumpsuit but does not seem to cut the skin beneath. The woman shouts something. Her face is red and angry, and she tries to grip her fellow prisoner's arm to restrain him. The man resists her, breaking free. He takes a few steps back and waits ready, bending at the waist, arms raised in front of himself. The woman spins around to face 812-3. The other prisoners move unsteadily, some forward, some back.

812-3's movements are almost graceful. They are calculated. He drives the palm of his left hand into the woman's face just as she turns to look at him again. She is the prisoner closest to him, and she takes the blow hard. She crumples. She cups her hands around her nose, and then her eyes roll back into her head and she collapses.

The tattooed prisoner lunges forward over the woman's head. He overreaches, swinging his weapon wildly. 812-3 grips his arm and twists roughly. The man's arm appears to disconnect at the elbow. As if he is unable to register the pain or his injury, the man still stumbles forward into the *robotnik*. He raises his working arm and claws at 812-3's face. The scrapes he leaves behind are sickly pale, but not bloody, on 812-3's skin.

The rest of the prisoners calculate their odds to be better as a group and they charge 812-3, kicking and punching. The prisoners pursuing their recreation at the other end of the gymnasium find it hard to ignore the fight now. They begin to wander near. None of them look ready to join the fight yet. They are watching, sometimes shouting. 812-3 appears overwhelmed at first by the number of blows he is receiving. He retreats a few steps, covering his head. When his head is covered, the attacking prisoners aim at his stomach, driving their knees into his diaphragm and jabbing at his midsection. 812-3 retreats a few steps farther. Then, reaching his limit, he straightens, rearing up and causing his most immediate opponents to stumble back.

812-3 rushes forward, his head down and his arms swinging wildly. He steps over the fallen woman as he runs pell-mell into the crowd. Men fall back from his charge with bloody noses and swollen eyelids. 812-3 does not stop even as the other prisoners fall still, gasping, holding themselves to alleviate the pain. Even when they stand motionless, 812-3 grinds his fist into their heads and drives his knee into their crotches.

The emergency lights—red and frantic—are blinking along the ceiling of the gymnasium. A guard runs into the gymnasium and calls for backup into the comms at his wrist. He points his gun at the crowd, which is already dispersing. Men and women limp to the walls. They place their hands against the metal and press their cheeks into the walls. When there is only one man left facing 812-3, the *robotnik* still does not stop. He crosses with his right hand and crushes the cheek and bones of the last opponent. The man's neck twists at an odd angle, and he falls, knees and then head, to the gymnasium floor.

Shouting, the guard approaches the *robotnik*. When he sees the other prisoner fall, his neck potentially broken, the guard fires his stun gun at 812-3. 812-3's arms fly out to his sides and his body shudders. One bolt and then a second. Teeth clenched and legs spasming, 812-3 falls. The guard kneels into his back and fastens his hands behind his back with a zip tie.

Just as Aiya realizes that she is holding her breath, the captain turns the video off. The monitor splits again into four screens, four feeds.

"Three prisoners in ICU. At least one probably won't last the day."

Aiya swallows. "Appeals aren't based on good behavior." Her lips feel numb.

The captain laughs in disbelief. "First words out of your mouth? Really?"

She dips her head, stares a moment at her lap. She has clasped her hands together so tightly that the circulation is cut off. Her knuckles are white.

"What do you want me to say?"

"You're not a public defender. Not here. Drop the case. Even if you could get this abomination a new trial, it doesn't deserve one."

She places one hand on the captain's desk and presses it into the wood so that it lies still. "He was attacked first."

"What? With that shiv? As if that could even really hurt it? Grunts don't live and die like we do. Unless you're talking a direct and crushing blow to the skull, it walks away unhurt. That—" He waves his finger at the monitor. It shows the main street of the settlement, the outside of the drilling facility, and the prison. "That is an act of unmitigated, unbalanced aggression. Unsafe by any measure."

"He was attacked." She can only repeat the words. Inside, she is screaming.

"What kind of bitch are you?" He looks at her, face grim, his eyes narrowed. "You see that and you still plan on representing it in court?"

"Not worried about being impolitic anymore?"

The captain stands. He is a large man with broad shoulders and strong arms. Instinctively, she shrinks back into her chair. She tries to think whether she has any protective device in her bag. But she is not in an alley in the Americas with a taser to hand.

"I need you to listen to me." It is not a need, but a demand. "That thing is not human. UN or no, we have the right to make decisions that protect humanity. Humanity." He repeats the last word with emphasis, each syllabus almost a word of its own.

"That is what I am trying to do, sir." Without thinking, she defers to his title. Her only concern now is to leave the room.

"Drop the case. I don't think I need to reason this with you any longer. It's an insult." The captain wears a gun at his belt and Aiya is not sure if it is lethal or stun.

"The appeal is already in processing. The First Circuit Court is considering precedents." She stands up and grips her bag under her arm. "I am sorry to disappoint you, captain."

"I'll forbid you access to the prison."

"That would violate rights provided him in the Articles." Her legs are weak beneath her.

He stares at her.

"Then maybe he'll kill you next. And maybe the guards won't hear until it's too late."

She smiles. She does not know how she can. "I've been threatened before. It's never worked." She does not let him know how much she wants to drop the case, how much she wants to lock herself into her bedroom and never walk the tunnel to the prison again.

He does not answer. The door slides open behind her and he sinks back into his chair. "You enjoy your day, Ms. Ritsehrer," he says. His voice is even and cold. "You've certainly ruined mine."

She does not nod or say goodbye. She exits quickly, hardly looking at the clerk as she makes her way to the street. The street is quiet. Most people are at work, based on a workday that approximates that of Earth. The artificial light is bright. Once she has moved far enough away from the district's governmental offices, she steps close to the wall of a small domicile. She slumps down, her legs folding underneath her. She clasps her bag close to her chest and buries her face in its canvas. She tells herself to breathe, in and out, in and out. Her lungs, constricted in panic, struggle with the lower concentration of oxygen in the open streets of the settlement. For a moment, her vision narrows. She closes her eyes. She breathes. She feels the wall at her back and the hard street under her feet. She breathes and tries to forget all that she has seen.

Contaminants appeared in new samples as well. Scientists considered the possibility that contaminants are not contaminants.

External Examination:

Autopsy begun at 0715 hours. The victim is an Asian male, measuring 165 centimeters, weighing 73.5 kilograms. Age is 29 years and external appearance is consistent. Incision across the throat is 13 centimeters with jagged edges . . .

Office of District Eta Coroner
Connie Pyles, M.D.
8.18.2144 CE

7.20.2145

The ice cavern presses close on Aiya as she walks home. She can feel it between the domiciles and the small buildings housing the commissary and doctors' offices, behind the thin transparent shield of the artificial atmosphere. The warmth of the artificial lights does not dispel the cold she feels. Her legs are still shaky under her.

Her watch pings and she checks the message there. It is from Peri. `It was leaked.` Aiya does not understand. She clears the messages and stops walking. A few men and women jostle by her, but she does not move. Her own domicile is not far from here, less than half a kilometer, but she cannot see it. The streets in the settlement are mapped to a close grid, bending back and forth rapidly She can hear something, though, a muffled chaos of raised voices and shouts. Then she realizes the import of Peri's message. She does not know whether to move forward or retreat. `Are you home,` she messages Peri.

`Crowd of people outside.` Which Aiya takes to mean that Peri is home.

She does not want to suspect the captain leaked the video of the prison fight because she wants to believe the laws she knows mean something here. She waits a moment longer, searching the network on her watch. She finds the video quickly. It was posted to the district's communal feed by an anonymous user. The anonymity is, in and of itself, suspicious, since users have to be registered to access the feed.

"Damn," she whispers under her breath.

As she starts walking again, she feels untethered. Even more than usual, she notices Europa's low gravitational pull. Her steps are long and loping. She cannot move as quickly as she wants to. She can hear people behind her, the soft crumble of gravel under their light steps. She glances back but she cannot tell from their faces whether they are heading to her home to join the crowd outside.

When she finally turns the bend that lets her see the small geodesic dome of her home, a small yellow flag waving atop it to indicate the number of people inside and their civilian status, she releases her breath in relief. The crowd is not as big as she imagined. Ten or fifteen people are gathered close around the door and the security camera is working hard to capture each of their faces, craning first one way and then another. Still. It is a crowd of people, angry from the sounds of them, who are blocking the entrance to the place where she eats and sleeps. Peri is inside.

I'm just outside, she messages Peri. But I don't think I can get through. Instinctively she moves into the thin shadow of another domicile, hoping the crowd will not notice her. But there are still those who are traveling close behind her. They pass by so near to where she stands that she can smell the military-grade shampoo used on their hair.

This is not fair. Peri's return message. Aiya almost laughs to herself. No. No, it is not. But that has been her catchphrase for the past two weeks. This is your fight. And Aiya realizes, feeling a bit sick to her stomach, that Peri is blaming her, calling her out, rather than the crowd or the leaked video. She does not know what to answer, so she clears the message without responding. She stares at the crowd. The newcomers glance back and see her face, her face that has been widely televised on both Earth and Europa.

"Hold up," one of them says, as if he is processing. Then he shouts. "She's here!"

She lifts her hands, almost as if she is surrendering. She searches out the right words. "I don't know why you're here, but I just want to enter my domicile. I'm not here to cause trouble."

"Too late," someone lost in the crowd rebukes her.

She turns her head, trying to search out the speaker. But all the faces seem similarly angry.

"My name is Aiya Ritsehrer." There is no point in hiding her name. They already know. "This is my home and I wish to go inside. Please disperse. Or I'm sure the police will be here soon to do it for you." Her fingers tremble and she slowly lowers her hands. She hopes that Peri has contacted the authorities. Though the captain's surveillance system should already have made him aware of the situation.

"*Robot*-lover!" It is a slur she has never heard before. It feels both old and new.

"Love. Hate. They have nothing to do with this situation." She is surprised her voice sounds so calm and carries so far. Her courtroom training is standing her in good stead. "You don't have to love me either. I just want to go inside." *The slur of what you love.*

"It killed one of our own." The woman who spoke is dressed in the patched jumpsuit of the drilling operations. "You defend it, you attack us."

"I am sorry for the loss of Derrien Cho." Aiya drops her head. "I am sorry there is no place safe from that, from murder." *If there is other sentient life on Europa, yet to be discovered or dug up, what will they think of us?* "But human is as human does. Not all of our instincts are good." She lifts her chin again. She tries to meet as many of their eyes as possible. She accuses them. "Please go away. If not for my sake, for the sake of my partner. She didn't sign up for this." In fact what she had signed dictated shared property and emergency contacts, but little else.

"It's not human."

She nods her head, neither agreeing nor disagreeing, just acknowledging the claim, the evergreen argument.

"The police are coming," Peri's voice is soft and frightened. She has opened the door just a crack, not even enough to disarm the security system. There is no need to say they will be here soon. It is a small place, District Eta.

The crowd begins to fray at the edges as members slip between the houses or jog off down the road. But there is a core of protesters remaining.

"I don't recognize any of you," Aiya says. She does know some of them, though. She recognizes the pharmacist from the medical offices, the commissary guard. But she means that she will not identify any of them. And that they do not seem like the people she knows.

A siren shrieks above her head, signaling that the roads of the settlement be cleared for the police. They are coming then. Aiya was not sure they would.

"Why?" The pharmacist grabs her arm. His face is very close to hers. She can see the pores of his skin on his nose and cheeks. More of the mob is dispersing. They jostle the two of them, and Aiya is shoved closer to the pharmacist. She can smell his sweat. She is afraid again. But she tries not to let it show.

"None of your fucking business." It takes all her breath to say it. He releases her arm. He is shuffled off with another protester. But he looks at her still, craning his neck. He seems confused, but his mouth is locked in a grimace. He makes a crude gesture just as he is dragged out of her sight by his companion.

Peri opens the door more widely. She is wearing a wrap dress, but it has been tied hastily so that it covers her more below than above. Aiya reaches forward and absently tugs the dress closed. Peri slaps her hand away. She cranes her neck to see whether all the protestors are gone.

"I told you," Peri whispers, her lips tight.

"You told me there'd be riots," Aiya repeats slowly, and she remembers it's true as she says it.

There are tears standing in Peri's eyes. She is angry. "You didn't listen."

She turns and goes back inside. Aiya waits a moment, reluctant to follow. Her neck prickles with sweat and anxiety.

"Peri." She steps inside. The door closes behind her with a gentle hiss. The air is cool inside, regulated by an individual thermostat. "It will be alright."

The sirens grow quiet and then disappear. Aiya hears nothing outside. If the police are still interested in the riot, they have begun to pursue the individual protestors. No one asks for permission to enter their domicile. No one checks to see if they are safe.

"You didn't listen. At all." Peri's voice grows louder. "I sat across from you, and I told you. This was dangerous. This was stupid."

"I'm sorry, Peri." Aiya looks at her, standing stiff and rigid in the narrow hallway. The kitchen and dining area are to her right, the sleeping quarters and bathroom to the left. It feels small and claustrophobic. There were days of training, days to prepare them for this lifestyle and ensure that they were ready for the realities of living on Europa.

"What are you sorry for?"

"I didn't mean to create this stress for you."

Peri's eyes open a little bit as if surprised. "You're not going to stop. Even after this?"

Aiya thinks of the video, the captain's threats, and the pharmacist's ugly face. "I can't."

"That's bullshit," Peri says. She goes into her sleeping quarters. She does not storm or slam her door. She is very quiet.

"Peri." Aiya's voice is sad.

The air recyclers kick on and hum in the silent hallway.

CAMP JOURNAL, 8.17.2145
@ CRETE, GEYSER

They are afraid I will transmit data to Hazlo Corp. before they can confirm, so they had arguments and conversations in the rover for the whole day until the sun set.

Zeus saw Europa, the daughter of Phoenix, gathering flowers in a meadow with some nymphs and fell in love with her. So he came down and changed himself into a bull and breathed from his mouth a crocus.

Hesiod
Translated by Hugh G. Evelyn-White
1914 CE

7.25.2145

"I loved her." 812-3 cups his chin in his hands. He sits cross-legged on his cot. "She told me I did. I believed her."

Aiya rests her notebook on her knee. She leans her head back and rests it on the wall. She has a headache and her stomach is unsettled. She can hear the guard occasionally shift his stance outside the cell, his boots heavy on the metal floor. He is not there to protect her.

It takes her a moment to register what 812-3 has said. "What did you say?" Her notes are messy, a scrawl of the vague defenses 812-3 had offered for the prison fight. He did not seem to understand how the video might impact the judges' decision to entertain an appeal. Or, at least, he refused to engage in a discussion about it.

"I loved her."

The words sound odd in this setting from that mouth. Aiya straightens in her seat.

"Now you're listening," he says.

"A trick to get my attention?" She relaxes again. "You could just snap your fingers."

"No. I was telling the truth. Though it doesn't answer any of your questions."

"Is this pertinent to the case?" She retreats into formality. "We're here to prepare for the appeal—if we're granted a hearing. We shouldn't waste time." She realizes her disinterest is feigned, but she clings to it.

"She was Derrien Cho's spouse. I thought, when you first visited, that she had sent you."

Aiya does not say anything. Her brain stutters, then starts again, as she realizes the implications of what he is saying.

"Labor laws and their enforcement." He looks at her. "Two different things."

She shakes her head, struggling to follow his chain of thought.

"We each of us have codes, usually oral keys," he continues, slow and clear, "which bypass our self-control. They activate core directives. Follow. Don't question. Their use was deemed illegal. But that doesn't keep a lot of supervisors from using them when convenient."

Aiya poises her stylus over her notes. "Cho's spouse?"

He looks at her, and she fears she has pushed him too quickly. His face loses much of its animation. Then he takes her hand. Instinctively she tries to tear it away, but his grip is strong. His palm, though it feels almost like skin, is just a little too solid under her fingers, as if he is more girder than flesh beneath the epidermis. "Her name is Tafee."

Aiya notes the name with her free hand.

812-3 presses his thumb onto the face of her watch. The gesture activates the artificial lens in Aiya's right eye, a mandatory implant for Europan settlers. She usually avoids using it. It is too invasive and makes her feel seasick. "See for yourself," he says. His voice is uneven.

A series of video clips, most thirty seconds or less, play on the lens.

Tafee is a tall, angular woman with freckled skin. Her hair is thinning and she wears it tucked closely behind her ears. She is a woman with a prominent collarbone and defined cheekbones. Her eyelids are heavy with thick lashes, her eyes blue-gray. 812-3 has observed her with taxonomic thoroughness. She is waiting for someone just inside the airlock of the drilling operations. She studies her tablet and her forehead furrows. She has peeled her suit off to the waist and she is wearing a plain white T-shirt with an army emblem on the breast pocket. When she looks up and smiles at Derrien Cho, alive and breathing, she shows all her teeth and it is beautiful.

"It is the first time I saw her." Aiya hears 812-3, distant beyond the memory. Aiya is aware again of his tight grip on her wrist.

"Your room is small." Tafee stretches her arms. She is naked under the sheets on the bed. There is a hollow between her breasts that is very pale. Her face glistens with sweat. *"We shouldn't be doing this."* 812-3's hand, almost translucent compared to her ruddy skin, rests on her stomach. *"Maybe we're programmed to it."* She smiles, big and toothy, as if at a private joke. *"Why are you doing it?"* 812-3's voice is soft, almost a whisper. She turns her head and her hair falls over her cheek. Half of her face is hidden by the pillow. *"Because I wanted to. I was bored."* 812-3 withdraws his hand. Her face shifts, becomes more serious. She reaches her hand out to his face. *"I didn't re-alize you would be so real. I thought this would feel less like cheating. But it doesn't."* Her eyes are wet, but her smile re-

turns, close-lipped. *"Why? Do you love me, Eight?"*

Aiya's throat feels tight. Her head is beginning to ache, as it often does when she uses the artificial lens, but she ignores it. The image changes, skips ahead.

"Derrien, it's not like that," Tafee's voice hisses and is lost to the arching dome above. The ice walls of the mine's antechamber frame Derrien's dark hair. *"He's a damn robotnik, Tafee. He's not even human. How could you do this to me?"* His face is red. He looks at 812-3. *"You feel like a real boy now?"* 812-3 doesn't answer, and Derrien lunges toward him. He stumbles on the graveled floor. Tafee catches his arm. *"Stop it, Derrien. Stop it."* Derrien backhands her, connecting with her cheek. She makes a small noise, an intake of breath, and almost falls. *"Bitch,"* he says between gritted teeth. There is spittle on his lips. He wraps both hands around her throat. She is frightened. Her face is pale, and her eyes are frantic. She shouts something, the beginning of an alphanumeric code.

812-3 suddenly flings himself back on the cot. He curls in on himself. Aiya gasps as the video feed abruptly clears on her lens. Her fist is clenched and her eyes are hot.

"Did she order you—" She stops, catches her breath. She looks at him. "Did she order you? Did she use the code?"

"He was killing her." His voice still sounds remote, almost mechanical.

"But was it your choice?"

He moves slowly on the bed, uncurling his legs, straightening his back. He smooths the jumpsuit on his chest and legs. His face is calm. He studies her face. She looks back. She does not look away, demanding an answer.

"I loved her," he says.

She relaxes her clenched fist. She powers off the tablet and nods her head. "And what does that feel like? How do you know?"

"You don't know?"

She shrugs. "I wasn't asking about me. I was asking about you."

He stares down at his hands, turns his palm back and forth. "Like someone sees you."

She repeats it, as if she is unsure of what he said. Then she turns on the tablet again and writes the words down. He watches her writing. "You don't think you can remember?"

"I find it interesting. If that's what we're resting your defense on, when—or if—you get a new trial."

"What do you mean?"

For the first time, when she glances up at him, she sees something like fear or anxiety in his face.

"Killing for love. It's sympathetic. And if you were ordered to it, inescapable."

"I didn't say I was ordered to it."

"Didn't you?" She reads back her earlier transcription. Her shorthand is messy, probably indecipherable to anybody but herself. *"Bypass our self-control."*

"Please don't use that." His words are clipped and rapid.

"You don't want me to use our best defense?"

"I don't want you to hurt her."

Aiya stands up, tucks the tablet into her bag, and fastens it. "I won't betray your confidence if you ask me not to share this information. But it would be foolish not to use it. It's our only case. Any human would use it."

She is a little ashamed as she says it. She bangs on the door to signal that she is ready to leave.

"It doesn't matter, does it?" he asks as the door is opening. "She's still human. And I'm not."

"That's the question," she says as the guard ushers her out. "Do you want them to see you as human? Or as a monster?"

CAMP JOURNAL, 8.18.2145
@ CRETE, GEYSER

Left behind to keep camp. Doctors and technicians took rover and returned to district to discuss samples and retrieve further tools.

Exhibit No.1: 8mm drill bit, registered to the
geological survey team, bloodied . . .

Government's Proposed Exhibit List
Colony, Europa v. Worker-class, ID 812-3
6.11.2145 CE

7.28.2145

Watermarks are outdated and unnecessary in electronic
communication, but the First Circuit Court uses one
anyway. It lingers, ghostlike, an imitation of an older US
seal, in the background of the document Aiya receives.
It has been days since the rioters crowded around the
front door of the domicile. It is quiet now, but she still expects to hear shouts of anger. She listens and hears only
the hum of the recyclers. She sits up in bed to study the
document more closely. Her fingers are trembling, which
surprises her.

There are footsteps in the hall. She lifts her head, waiting to see if Peri will stick her head in. But the steps do not hesitate; they go into the kitchen.

The light in the room is dim. Rather than strengthening the brightness of her screen, she triggers the artificial sunlight, so that the whole room gradually fills with warm light. Finally, she forces herself to focus on the document itself. She skims past the officious greeting and the legalese of the first paragraph. She holds her breath until she sees the words. *Worker-class, ID 812-3, will be granted an appeal on 31 August 2145. Hearing will take place, by digital proxy, in the District Eta courts. Before that date, the petitioner will submit an appellate brief, outlining their argument.*

She drops her tablet onto the blankets and hides her face in her hands. Tears of relief are in her eyes. She gasps, trying to catch her breath. Swinging her legs out of bed, she shoves off the sheets. She goes into the kitchen. For a moment, Peri looks alarmed and Aiya forgets the tension and anger between them.

"Are you alright?" The eggs begin to burn in the skillet when Peri does not stir them.

"Great." She smiles. A shadow falls over Peri's face. "I'm sorry. I wanted to share."

Peri scrapes the bottom of the skillet with the spatula. "What?" She is bracing herself.

"First district accepted the appeal."

Peri nods her head. She does not raise her eyes from the eggs. "I assumed they would. You're good at what you do."

Aiya tries to smile. "It's good news, yeah?"

Peri shrugs. "The mob will be back," she says.

"But the government says yes now. Official endorsement. Now it's not me that's the problem."

Peri looks at her. There are bags under her eyes. "You don't really believe that. That it's all over. That people won't blame you."

Aiya tugs on her shirt, twists it close to her waist.

"When they partnered us." The words are coming fast, as if she has been waiting a long time to say them. "I was excited. We got along well. I thought, now I have someone that will watch out for me. Europa is a scary place, when you're boarding the shuttle to go and live there. Maybe to never come back to Earth."

Aiya thinks about reaching out her hand and touching Peri's arm. She doesn't. She holds herself very still.

"I didn't think then, back when I was excited"—Peri sets the spatula down on the counter, leaning against the molded ceramic—"that you would be the one to make it scary."

The eggs are burning and Aiya worries they will set off the smoke alarms. She thinks that she should take hold of the handle, throw the whole lot into the sink, but she cannot move. She knows what Peri will say next, and it is not surprising. She is not shocked. In some ways, she is relieved. But she feels frozen to the spot. The sadness is unexpected.

"I've requested a document of my own," Peri says. She takes a breath. She is on the edge of tears. Aiya can tell. "We should dissolve our partnership. There is a provision in place for temporary housing. I looked into it. After the protest." She wants to call it something else.

"You're leaving?" It is the talk of housing that surprises Aiya, though it is the natural extension of a dissolution of partnership.

"I think you should."

A shrill beeping sounds throughout the domicile. Sprinklers kick on, dousing the eggs, the stove, and both of them in a fire retardant foam. Peri turns off the burner. The eggs are crackling and brown. The beeping stops.

"If that's what you want," Aiya answers. She does not know what else to say. She does not even know if she should fight to stay in the domicile instead. Neither of them acknowledges their wet clothes or hair.

"Can you move today?" Peri's face is hard, though her eyes are hot and sparkling.

"I don't know." Aiya stutters a bit. "Yes. I guess."

"Good. Thank you." She smooths her hair with both

hands, remakes her ponytail. She looks relieved. Aiya almost feels happy for her, as if she is a third party, as if she is Peri's close friend and only wishes the best for her.

She leaves the kitchen and Aiya watches her go. The skillet pops as it adjusts to the sudden change in temperature.

"Not my mess," Aiya whispers as she leaves the kitchen herself, making a list in her head of what she needs to pack and what information she needs to obtain. The bot crosses paths with her, red light aglow, intent on cleaning the wet floor. It chirrups angrily when she knocks into it.

CAMP JOURNAL, 8.19.2145
@ CRETE, GEYSER

I can last in the cold without a suit for short periods of
time. I tested my limits today, walking out to the geyser
and back.

We, the Congress of the Americas, do grant, with the support of the people, a charter of colonization to the Hazlo Corporation, to be enacted under the direct jurisdiction and supervision of the executive, legislative, judicial, and military branches of the Americas, for the purpose of advancing scientific knowledge, and to be located in the northern hemisphere of Jupiter's moon Europa . . .

Charter of colonization
Signed by Prime Minster Cartere
and Members of Congress
2115 CE

5.14.2144

The first thing that Aiya saw when the ship released them from their seats and opened wide the bay doors was a bank of elevators. They stood independent of walls and building. It was a concrete floor and a row of elevator cars like metallic pills, slightly ovoid, enough to throw off her Earthan expectations. She found out later that they were called shuttles, not elevators. But they moved up and down through a tunnel of ice.

"Move forward," an inhuman voice repeated again and again over the ship's speakers. Peri shoved her from behind, encouraging her to follow the ship's instructions. So she did, grasping her travel bag close to her side. The sound of the offboarding passengers echoed around them in the empty hanger.

"Shuttles one, two, or three, depending on your visas," a soldier directed them as their shoes hit the concrete floor. Aiya glanced at Peri, and she mouthed a number to her.

The shuttle doors shut once it was filled to capacity. A video played on the walls, introducing the new settlers to the planet and to District Eta. She had imagined expanses of ice, a sweeping horizon of blue and white. There were glimpses, moments of the planet's surface, but the video concentrated primarily on the settlement, buried kilometers below the surface of the planet, just off shore, if one counted dams and walls of ice as shore, of the planet's submerged sea. The aerial shot showed a labyrinth of narrow streets, lined with geodesic domes.

Colorful flags atop the domes separated the settlement into sectors by civilian and military status, by occupation and rank. Peri grabbed her hand and squeezed it.

"But where's Europa?" Aiya asked. Peri laughed.

Someone behind them, since they were all packed close in the shuttle, chimed in. "We're looking for alien life but imagine if they found us first, buried under the surface of their own planet. Surprise!" Aiya imagined, from the shifting behind her, that the speaker had made an enthusiastic hand gesture.

"You forget that it's our planet now." Aiya pointed to the flags on the domes, the logos on the doors of the elevator. "They'd be trespassing."

The person behind them thought that she was joking and laughed accordingly. She wasn't sure if she was joking herself, and Peri could sense her hesitation. "It'll be good," she said.

The elevator released them into a narrow corridor or alley of ice. She could see it opening wide ahead, and the light there was warm and yellow like the sun of home. Peri took a small packet from a soldier. It corresponded again with their visas. There was an address—or something approximating it, a spot on the grid—marked in bold black letters.

"Just like that?" Aiya looked at the packet and then again down the tunnel. "We're home?"

"Come on." Peri led the way. She walked with confidence, despite the decreased gravity, and the light grew around her as she disappeared up ahead. But Aiya could not make her legs move. She was struggling to remember why she had traveled seven hundred million kilometers or more through space. To get away from people? And yet everything here, from the artificial sunlight to the domes, smacked of human bureaucracy. There was no frontier here.

"Forward, not back," the soldier barked at those who were lingering. Aiya felt personally reprimanded.

She shuffled forward, each step lighter than she expected, until she had cleared the alley and was staring at a wall of domes. Beyond the initial row, she could see domes of varying sizes, larger ones to house the commissary and other offices, smaller ones to house the partners and families arriving to settle here. District Eta was fairly young, and there was a crisp, sharp feel to the graveled pathways, to the strategically placed plants, to the arc of the dome above. It was ice, above and below, separated from the settlement by a carbon polymer bubble that molded itself to the carved dome. It felt fragile and everlasting at the same time.

Peri had turned and was waiting for her. "Good things, Aiya. Think good things." And she smiled, broad and big, as only she could.

CAMP JOURNAL, 8.20.2145
@ CRETE, GEYSER

Quake disrupted gyroscope. I took the day to rest and
recalibrate.

Robotnici have revolutionized the way we do business, reducing workplace injury and making the impossible possible.

Infomercial, Americas

2092 CE

7.28.2145

"Shouldn't have brought you with me," Aiya mutters to the bot. It is trying to work out the dimensions of her new room in order to optimize its cleaning route. It seems angered by the sudden change in environment. The red light has been on, unblinking and insistent, for the last hour. Aiya steps around it with an armload of folded shirts and pants. The decision to take the bot was last minute and probably a spiteful one.

"Small," the bot chirps, as if realizing that Aiya now has only one room to her name. Her new quarters are supposedly short-term, a room with en suite kitchen and bathroom in what can best be understood as an embassy, a place for temporary American visitors or foreign diplomats to stay until they leave or are transferred to permanent quarters. Permanent quarters are reserved, however, for groups of two or more.

She stores the last of her clothes and sets up her tablet and files on the table by the bed. The sheets and blankets on the bed are standard issue, rough and scratchy to the touch.

"Small," the bot repeats.

"I get it." She falls back onto the bed. "No need to rub it in."

The bot bumps against the molded plastic of the bed frame. It squeaks, more high-pitched and irritated than any noise she has heard from it before. She drops her hand over the side of the bed and absentmindedly looks for a power switch on the dome of the bot. It shrugs away from her hand. She rolls over on her side to look at it.

"You want something else to do," she says, "try your hand at this brief."

The deadline for the brief is not far off, a matter of days rather than weeks. Unconventional, but clearly the first district judges want this appeal off their plates as soon as possible. The morning, however, has been spent in moving her things out of her old domicile. Peri did not watch her go. Aiya was happy for it. She tells herself that she can seal off this part of her life on Europa and move on without consequences. She knows it is not true.

"Brief," the bot chirps as if it is a synonym for *small*.

She stares at the bot as it veers off toward the far corner of the room. It has an opaque shell, so its batteries, processors, and wires are shadows underneath the skin.

"Do you also want your freedom?" she asks it. The room feels like a prison cell, despite the light, despite the circulating air, despite the monitor embedded in the wall and programmed to circulate images of fields and woods and seas from Earth.

The bot pauses, spins, focuses its light on her. It is only a second, and then it turns to explore the far wall again.

"I'm going crazy," she whispers, but she continues to watch it. Her eyes sting. She does not look away.

The bot bumps its way toward the closed door and stops there, red light flickering. Then, after a moment, it continues on its route. There is not far to go.

CAMP JOURNAL, 8.21.2145
@ CRETE, GEYSER

The geyser was active today and the water crystallized and froze as it fell. At the mouth of the geyser, I saw unusual movement, not water. I saw nothing when I went close.

In space, we are free. We are free because the circumference of our movement is restrained. Our questions and our choices are limited. And yet we have a purpose, a purpose wherein even the first step is weighted. And so, in space, we will have no prisons. We will have no crime.

Brandøn Wrightgard
The Stars Will Reach for Us:
A New Philosophy for a New Age
2087 CE

8.3.2145

Europa, from orbit, is beautiful. Though Aiya cannot shake the notion that it looks like a frosted glass lens scratched and stained by overuse. It is white and brown and green at different glances. She stands silent at the picture window of the station, watching the planet, and only moves when a waiter brings her a beverage on a silver tray.

"Thank you." She sips the drink. It is a cocktail. She can tell there is either absinthe or arak in the mix. It is one of the few alcoholic beverages she can stand the taste of. But it has an extremely high alcohol content, so she drinks it slowly, nursing it. Water condenses on the glass and drips on her fingers.

"I hope you like it. The bar said it was the only drink you had ordered before." The speaker is a woman. She has short hair cut close to her scalp and delicate piercings at her eyebrow. She is wearing something akin to a formal jumpsuit. At first, she does not look at Aiya directly.

"Ambassador O'Donnell?" Aiya takes a guess at the woman's name. The ambassador nods.

"I'm happy you accepted my invitation to spend a day or two on the station. It's a different experience from the settlements. And it seemed you might need some time to clear your head."

Aiya tries to smile, but she is nervous. She sets the drink down on the lip of the window and imagines she can feel the press of space just on the other side of the glass. The ship she traveled in from Earth to Europa possessed none of the elegance of the permanent station orbiting the moon.

"I appreciated it," she says and waits for the ambassador to say more.

"It's not usually my place"—O'Donnell nods toward the surface of the planet below—"to deal with domestic matters. And, ultimately, this appeal on behalf of Worker-class, ID 812-3 is a domestic matter."

"But?"

The ambassador laughs. She makes a gesture with her hands as if to compliment Aiya on her perceptiveness. She turns slightly toward her to establish an intimacy between them. "But Earth is watching. Not just the Americans. The UN is watching. Everyone is watching to see what we decide. Even here, on Europa, three nations represented. AI and human, are we peers or not?"

She shrugs her shoulders and finally looks Aiya in the eye. Aiya does not answer right away. She remembers 812's face when she had announced the basis for her appeal, the slight sense of unease that indicated greater upset beneath the surface.

"After all, if humans are not peer to AI, if we are not sufficient to serve as jury, then what effect does that have on past UN measures?" The ambassador crosses her arms. She turns her gaze away, pretends to study Europa's surface, but Aiya can tell that she is listening very closely.

"The question is not really one of equality." Aiya speaks slowly, stepping carefully. "Or rather, it's not a question of reversing UN decisions on AI rights. It's a matter of prejudice. A prejudiced jury is an unfair jury. The question is whether a human jury is an unbiased jury in this case."

"I took some law classes myself in college," the ambassador answers. Aiya waits to hear the relevance of the statement. "It still seems to me," she continues, "that the appeal poses some real threat to AI rights overall, despite your best intentions."

Aiya closes her hands together, squeezes them tight. She has had doubts herself. One step forward, two steps back. But her concern is for her client, not a cause.

"Does he see it that way?" At first, Aiya thinks the ambassador has read her thoughts.

"He trusts me to do what is best in the case."

The ambassador shrugs her shoulders as if shifting an uncomfortable coat. "I've never liked that. Someone trusting me to do for them. Do it yourself. That's what I say."

Aiya does not point out the contradiction between who the ambassador is and what she says. "Did the Eta captain of police speak with you?"

"Yes." The ambassador grips her elbow. She reads Aiya's face and smiles apologetically. "He's horrible, isn't he? I don't want you to think I'm speaking on his behalf here. My concern is strictly for the image. What's the picture here, Ms. Ritsehrer?"

"I don't know." Aiya looks at the window, at the moon framed there.

"Well." The ambassador's sigh is pointed. "Enjoy the

amenities." She waits a moment longer with Aiya, staring out with her. "Enjoy it from the outside for a while longer."

Aiya bends her head and nods a little. She is tired of finding the right words. The ambassador finally leaves, her shoes padding softly on the brushed metal floor. Aiya looks at her drink and considers picking it up again. Instead, she opts to return to her room and take a hot bath, a rare luxury in the settlement where water was so carefully monitored and meted out.

The ritual of filling the tub, checking the temperature, smelling the different bath salts experimentally is an old and familiar one. It reminds her of Earth. It reminds her of what it feels like to be safe, free even from the nagging undercurrents of anxiety she usually ignores. Free from fearing what might happen if the artificial atmosphere failed, if the ice groaned and split above her, if the mob ignored the rule of law.

She sinks into the water slowly, and she almost sobs as the warmth envelops her up to her shoulders. She rests her head on the edge of the tub and stares up into the window inset into the ceiling. There are stars there. No moon. No planets. Only stars, small, silver, violently bright points of light.

Scientists returned at end of day. I made them meals. They were very quiet. They have brought back video recording gear with them.

The use of force on AI prisoners (defined here as: stun guns, bolts, tasers) is allowed at the discretion of the officer. If a weapon is discharged, the officer must report to prison administration as soon as is conveniently possible and may be referred to a licensed therapist for evaluation.

Training Manual for Correctional Officers
District Eta Department of Corrections
2140 CE

8.24.2145

"Are you ready?" Aiya asks 812-3.

"Yes." He does not treat the question as rhetorical in the slightest. "But you'll be doing most of the talking. Are you ready?"

She smiles, breathes deeply, remembering her old mantras. Project confidence to the client. "Of course.

Just one more day and we'll be on to the real work. The new trial."

He crosses his legs underneath himself. He is quiet when she mentions the trial and he picks at the blanket with two fingers pinched closely together. She clears her throat. She feels irrationally guilty.

"But we can plan that later. One step at a time." She looks at him, hoping that this will put him at ease. "I wanted you to see the final form of the submitted brief." She hands him her tablet. He moves slowly to take it. "The profile of the jury. The animus in the community. That's all in there."

She watches him read, suddenly aware of the dim light in the cell and how cold it is. The chair is hard and uncomfortable. She tries to imagine 812-3 warm and affectionate and lying uncovered in a bed, much as he remembered Tafee. But here, washed out by the dim strip lights, his cheeks sunken, his skin almost translucent, she cannot imagine him any other way than he is now.

"I don't understand some of the language." He hands the tablet back. "I understand the words," he adds quickly. "I don't understand the way they're used here."

"Legalese." She almost smiles. Even with a computer for a brain, 812-3 finds legal language confusing. "A universal annoyance."

"Using words to hide, to confuse, to say the opposite of what you mean. To lie." His face is pinched and she does not know if she is imagining the purple hollows under his eyes.

"I'm not sure that's unique to my profession."

"No." He looks at her. "Will we win?"

She has no choice now, no choice but to speak simply. "I don't know. But I think there's a chance."

"Supposing the prejudice is not inherent in the system."

She leans back. "It sounds like you've been reading."

"Books will rehabilitate me, yes?" He lowers his head. He lays his hands very deliberately on his legs, each finger spread apart from the others.

She swallows. "812—"

"To restore, to make healthy again, to make live again." He rattles off the definitions, interrupting her. "Should I have let you do that instead? That's what you wanted to do."

"I wanted to help."

"Help? Help me?" He shifts to the edge of the cot. He does not move his hands. His body is tense. "And how would you have made me live again?" There is a break in his voice.

She looks at him. She clutches her own hands nervously to her stomach.

"She didn't do that," he says. He is studying her posture. His words are hollow and slow, low-ringing.

Aiya tries to force her arms and fingers to relax. "I do want to help you." She makes sure to repeat each word deliberately.

"What do you think I would do to you? If there were no guards? What makes you shrink back?"

"You killed a man." She doesn't want to say it, but it comes out anyway. She is tired. She is scared. And sometimes she cannot distinguish of who or why.

He smiles, but the rest of his face hardly moves. His eyes are wide and dark. "But I'm not human. We don't put men on trial for the animals they kill. Different species."

She looks at the door and thinks about standing up or calling for the guard. She wonders if the guard would deign to hear her.

"Isn't that our argument?" And he is growing quiet again. He pulls his legs back up on the bed and pushes himself close to the wall. "We are not peers."

"But it wasn't really you, was it?" She tries to push past the hoarseness in her voice. She needs him to admit it. She needs to know that the loss of her home, the loss of Peri, the loss of her community aren't for nothing.

"You want me to admit that I'm a slave. At the core of who I am. You want me to say she used me."

She rests her elbows on her knee, presses her forehead into her hands. Her face is hot.

"You want to take her away from me." He is almost whispering. His voice is softening.

After so many visits, she is still afraid of him. And she is angry at herself. Her throat hurts. "I am sorry," she says. She repeats it. "I am sorry."

He is quiet. She counts the seconds, the minutes, to herself. Finally, she pushes herself up. She shoves her hair roughly back from her face. He is looking at her. "I don't know why you're here," he says.

"Because you asked." It is the only answer she has. She is not sure what it's worth. She is not sure if it's even true.

"Why are you on Europa? You weren't shipped here in a cargo hold."

She takes a deep breath. "Because I hoped there was something more than human here."

"Is there?" His hair reflects back the light. She doesn't know how his heart works or if he needs to breathe. At some point, she probably saw a documentary or a commercial video about *robotnici* physiology.

"I don't know." In the stale air and dim light, she cannot call to mind the hypothetical aliens they'd talked of on Earth. She can barely remember the outdoor café where she first talked to Peri.

He nods. He looks suddenly small and frail, though

he is not. She wants to put a hand on his shoulder or in his hair. She also wants, some small part of her wants, to never see him again.

"Tomorrow, then," he says. He glances at each of the cell walls, at the door, at the low ceiling and the lights. He is measuring something. She does not know, cannot know, what.

CAMP JOURNAL, 8.23.2145
@ CRETE, GEYSER

A camera was set up to observe the geyser. A probe was released into the mouth of the geyser to measure temperature and take pictures.

The first Europan missions were not as successful as Prime Minister Cartere's administration had wished. As a result, his proposal to grant a charter for a Europan colony to the Hazlo Corporation was met with skepticism . . .

A History of the First Europan Colony
2174 CE

8.25.2145

The single courtroom in District Eta is utilitarian. It is housed in the basement level of the government offices, and the lighting is almost as poor as in 812-3's cell. He is here, escorted in by two guards, and dressed in an ill-fitting suit. Aiya wonders where he got it. The district clerk slides in behind him and moves to the communication array behind the judge's bench. She is muttering under her breath. An unidentified *robotnik* travels close behind her, carrying a bulky amplifier that will boost their signal from beneath the surface of Europa to the orbiting station, and from there to Earth. The relayed messages may take as long as an hour to travel to Earth.

Aiya waits for 812-3 to be led to her side. The guards remove the restraints on his wrists. They look at her, grim and disapproving, before returning to stand guard at the door to the room.

"You understand there will be a delay," the clerk says as she turns on the monitor and enables it to receive messages. "It will make for highly unconventional procedure. Some formalities will be abbreviated." She directs the *robotnik* to set down the amplifier. "After all, you don't want to be waiting an hour for each hello and goodbye."

"No," Aiya agrees. "Thanks for your help."

The clerk shrugs off her thanks. The district attorney enters the room and glances around at everyone there. "All present for the circus?" He smirks a little. He takes his seat across from Aiya and pulls up his brief on his tablet. His hair is disheveled and he looks as if he just rolled out of bed. She tries to give him the benefit of the doubt. It is early, the better to maximize their time given the communication delays. Luckily, the artificially constructed day and night beneath the surface of Europa aligns their work day with that of the American east coast.

The first message from the judges catches them both by surprise. The clerk steps rapidly back from the monitor and Aiya realizes that the message has already begun or was started in the middle of a sentence.

"—for gathering here today. We have read the briefs that you sent us and we are prepared to pursue the oral hearing in the following manner. We would like to hear any further arguments from the appeal attorney, Ms. Ritsehrer, and the district attorney, Mr. Hertz. A statement from the appellant, if desired, is also welcome. You will send these as one message so we may hear and weigh the evidence alongside your briefs and decide on any further questions we may have. These questions will be sent in a following message. The court thanks you for your patience and reminds you that there is a media presence in the courtroom here. We await your statements."

The three judges, two men and one woman, are solemn-faced, and their white collars—the only remaining element of the judicial dress code—stand out starkly on the pixelated screen. The screen blinks and their faces are gone.

The clerk is situating a camera for the video feed on the judge's bench. "Give me one second," she asks. The *robotnik* hovers nearby, her appearance that of a thin woman. She is staring at 812-3.

"Make your case," Hertz says, his voice tired. He tilts

his chair onto its back legs. The informality of the proceedings makes Aiya uneasy. She turns away from Hertz and waits for the clerk to give her the go-ahead. She practices her delivery in her head, running over her main points and reviewing, one last time, the questions and discussion during jury selection of the original trial.

"Okay," the clerk sighs softly. She eyes Aiya to see if she is ready. Aiya nods.

"Your Honors." Aiya reminds herself to smile slightly, but not so big as to make light of the situation. "Thank you for your time." She imagines the journalists on Earth, their recorders at the ready for the receipt of this communication. She replays the warning of the ambassador on the space station and can almost taste the arak on her tongue. "We make our appeal today on the most basic, the most fundamental, of rights for any person on trial in an American court. One that was written into the very constitution of our former United States and—so important—preserved in the Articles of our current nation. The right to a jury of your peers. A right that guarantees an unbiased evaluation of the defendant."

She takes a breath. Hertz makes a noise, but she refuses to look at him. "We are here today, if it please the court, to say—" She pauses and then takes 812-3's arm. She brings him into the focus of the camera. "We are here today to say that no single jury member in Colony, Europa v. Worker-class, ID 812-3, viewed this *robotnik* as a peer, and therefore the court failed to provide him his constitutional rights under the Robot Rights Act of 2141."

The words are dry, legalistic. This case, win or lose, is groundbreaking. It will be precedent. It will be cited in legal journals. It is only now, as she blinks into the camera, that she fully realizes the import of the case, caught up as she has been in understanding 812-3 himself.

She lowers her head and consults her tablet. She has highlighted the portions of the jury selection process she wants to repeat in the hearing. She squares her shoulders and begins, citing every piece of evidence she has that speaks to bias in the court proceedings. When she is done, she feels empty and she sits down. She gestures to 812-3, indicating he can speak if he wants to. He stands up, looks at the clerk, perhaps the *robotnik* beside her. The *robotnik* stands unnaturally still, a bead of condensation dripping from her hairline to her jaw.

"I want to go back to work," he says, very quietly. Then he sits back down. The clerk waits, staring at him, expecting him to say something further. When he does not, she reangles the camera. Hertz stands up, cracking his back as he does so. He begins his own statement, loud and clear, but Aiya cannot focus on what he is saying.

She tries to catch 812-3's eye. "Why?" she whispers. He does not act as if he hears her.

She rests her chin in her hand and tries to be calm. She tries to focus on the statement of the appellee.

It is a long day. After the first statements have been recorded, the clerk transmits them to Earth. While they wait, Aiya searches out coffee. Hertz disappears and comes back freshly shaved. 812-3, still under watch, does not move from his seat.

The questions from the judges are not entirely unexpected. *What were the professions of the jury members?* To establish some other basis for defining peer relations. *Was Worker-class, ID 812-3, harassed while on stand?* To establish whether the claimed bias extended to the court at large. *Was Worker-class, ID 812-3, harassed or abused while in holding?* To establish the community from which the jury was chosen.

She has answers prepared for these questions. Hertz has the objections and counterpoints that she anticipated. He is the one who finds a way to bring up the fight and the injured prisoners, despite its occurrence after the trial in question. She wonders whether she should have gotten ahead of that and contextualized it herself. The wounds that 812-3 could show for his pains are still visible, though he is a quick healer, but she knows he will not show them if she asks.

"Ultimately," she says in her closing statement, the last one allowed by the judges, who looked tired in their last message, "we are not here to establish whether we find 812-3 frightening or intimidating, whether we engage in prejudice ourselves." She pauses, lets the silence speak to her condemnation of Hertz and the district. "We are here to decide whether 812-3 was given a fair trial by a jury of his peers. I think that I have convincingly argued that he was not in my brief and in my statements here today."

Here is an odd term for their circumstances, a court room divided by space, stars and planets. She looks into the camera and tries to imagine that she is looking into the faces of the judges. She knows the face of her closing statements. She used to practice it in her mirror. She is more familiar with presenting it to a jury. She does not know if her combination of conviction and request will work on the judges.

"What time is it?" Hertz asks when he finishes his statement. The clerk is confirming coordinates of the message, as she has done so many times today.

"1700," the clerk answers. She rolls her head onto one shoulder and then the next. "End of the work day."

They have to stay anyway, for almost two hours, as they wait for the judges' reply. It is brief. The judges will deliberate and the court will reconvene at ten o'clock the next morning. Hertz mutters something under his breath as the message fades to black. The clerk unplugs cords at the bench, and the *robotnik* holds out her arms to take the more expensive pieces of equipment.

812-3 does not get up until all three have left the room. The guards shift their feet and one loudly removes the restraints for the *robotnik* from his belt. The cuffs click ominously in the quiet.

"Can I live in a cell forever?" She does not know if he is asking her or himself. The question does not seem rhetorical.

"Have some faith," she says. She slips her tablet into her bag and adjusts the bag on her shoulder.

"I am *robotnik*." He says it as if he is identifying a nationality or an ethnicity. She is not sure of the objection implicit in the answer. Perhaps he is saying that he cannot have faith. That he is not programmed to believe.

"You speak for them all here. That is what you are doing."

He shakes his head. He holds out his hands for the restraints as the guards grow impatient and step forward to interrupt their conversation. "Do not make me one of many. I am just one. Differentiated by number. 812-3."

She nods and tries to understand. "Just wait until tomorrow before you give up hope."

He does not look at her as he is led away.

CAMP JOURNAL, 8.24.2145
@ CRETE, GEYSER

The scientists are divided on the nature of the life that we have found here. Xi asked if there was something more than microorganisms to study.

In closing, members of the jury, I ask you to consider this. You are a woman and you have traveled with your spouse to a colony far from your home, far from everything you know. All you know, all you have, is your spouse. And then your spouse is torn away from you, killed violently by a grunt, which—through some hardware, software, some *malfunction*—considers your partner a threat. Would you be frightened? Would you be angry?

Statement of the prosecution
Colony, Europa v. Worker-class, ID 812-3
6.24.2145 CE

8.25.2145

It is close to curfew, a curfew rarely enforced, when Aiya

steps out into the street. The air is cool and the light is dimming, both artificial approximations of night on Earth. The dome of the sky looks less real than it does during the day, the striated colors of twilight too distinct. She tugs her jacket close and checks the address again on her watch, a street and domicile number not far from her own temporary housing. Her stomach rumbles, because she has not eaten yet since returning from the courtroom. No food sounds appealing.

There are not many people on the streets. Their quiet conversations mingle with the murmur of the street-cleaner bot who will spend the night roaming up and down each street on the grid. She watches the bot pass her by and studies the blinking red lights she has come to think of as eyes on her own small bot. It does not notice her. She shakes her head, stuffs her hands into her pockets, and picks up her pace.

The domicile's flag indicates a civilian household with trained labor occupants. There are ferns in white planters at the door, the leaves curled in on themselves at the end of day. She waits for the camera to read her face and alert the resident to her identity and presence. It is quiet. She does not hear anyone moving. Perhaps Tafee does not want to speak to her. She lifts a hand and knocks on the door. Aiya is not sure why Tafee should want to talk to her. The answer she hopes to hear is damning.

"Who are you? What do you want?" The speaker crackles. The question, to a certain extent, is rhetorical. The scan would have given her Aiya's name and occupation in the settlement.

"Ms. Johanssen. My name is Aiya Ritsehrer. I'm an attorney."

A pause on the other side of the door. "I know that. But why are you here?" As if the original questions—who and why—are one and the same thing.

"I want to ask you a few questions." Aiya bites her lip and takes a chance. "On behalf of 812-3." She does not use his full designation.

One of the neighbors is entering his home. He looks at her, curious. She has not stopped to think that the appeal hearing has probably been broadcast live to the district.

"I'm sorry. Who?" But the voice is cautious, knowing.

Aiya tilts her head back, looks at the sky, tries to summon patience. "The *robotnik* convicted in the death of your husband." The words sound harsh spoken aloud. She feels them ringing in the street and is glad the neighbor has gone into his home.

The door slides open. It is odd to Aiya that she recognizes the woman without having ever met her. Freckled skin and fair, thinning hair. She is pretty, but she looks hungry, lean and desperate.

"I'm sorry for the loss of your husband," Aiya says,

convention rising to the surface.

Tafee does not acknowledge her sentiment. "Why are you really here?" Her voice is almost hoarse. "I've already been on the witness stand. I've talked with the police."

"Yes." Aiya tries to smile. "May I come in?"

Tafee holds an arm up across the entryway. "I don't think we have anything to talk about."

Aiya looks at her for a moment. She lowers her voice. "If you cared for him at all, may we talk for just a few minutes? Inside."

"Of course I cared for Derrien." She is ashamed as she says it. Aiya can tell. She has worked enough trials to tell. Tafee meets her eyes and something crumbles behind them. "Come in, then."

It is dark inside. Tafee does not turn on any lights. She leads the way into the living area. Everything is meticulously clean. The last light of evening filters in through partially closed blinds. She does not offer Aiya a seat, so they stand awkwardly, facing each other over a low futon.

"Say what you're here to say," she says. She crosses her arms and looks just to the side of Aiya's head.

"I won't beat around the bush." Aiya watches her. "You know that I have initiated an appeal on behalf of 812-3." She looks up to see Tafee confirm this with a reluctant nod. "If this appeal is successful, there will be a new trial. 812-3 is not responsible for the murder of your husband."

She feels, finally, sure as she says it. "Is he? Not really."

The color drains from Tafee's face. She looks almost as colorless as 812-3. "I don't know what you're trying to say."

Aiya nods and looks down at her hands. "He was hurting you. Maybe he would have killed you. I'm not judging you here. I just need the truth. 812-3, if he stays in prison, he's not going to win every fight. He's not going to survive the police outrage."

Tafee looks around her, as if searching out a seat. Rather than sitting on the futon, close to where Aiya is standing, she kneels on the ground. Aiya leans on the back of the futon, unwilling to turn away.

"We can make a case of self-defense. If it comes to that."

Tafee places a trembling hand over her mouth. Tears stand in her eyes. "I can't do what you're asking."

"Can't? Won't?"

"I'm not a murderer," she whispers.

"Neither is he."

Some internal mechanism in the wall—water filtration, air recycling—clicks on. Tafee looks up at Aiya. Her cheeks are flushed. She stutters over the first words.

"It's not the same, is it? He's not human."

Aiya straightens, her back rigid with sudden anger. Tafee continues, stumbling in her need to say all she wants to say. "That's the whole basis of your appeal, isn't it? We're not the same. You can't ask me to put my freedom and my life on the line for a *robotnik*."

Aiya finds it hard to speak, her throat is so tight. "You convinced him that he loved you."

"It's the same thing then, isn't it?" Desperation still in her face and in her voice. "Love is what you think it is. And that's not my fault. And I'm not responsible for what he did based on that feeling."

Aiya laughs once in disbelief. "That's how you've convinced yourself that what you did is alright? You knew his code. I don't know if he shared it with you, if Derrien told you, if you found out another way. But you knew it. He didn't have any choice."

Tafee covers her face in both hands. She sobs loudly. "This is illegal." She coughs. "You can't be here, doing this."

"You can't have it both ways," Aiya persists. "Is he human or isn't he? Did he have a choice or didn't he?"

Aiya doesn't move until Tafee's crying grows softer. She wipes her face with her sleeve and dabs under her eyes with her fingers. Her nose is red. She looks up again at Aiya. If there had been any remorse in the tears, it is now overshadowed by anger.

"You can't have it both ways either," she hisses.

Aiya smiles, lips pressed tight, trying to cover her own confusion.

"Leave my house," Tafee orders her. "Or I'll ping the police."

"He'll release his memories into record," she says, trying to keep her voice even and calm. "He'll do it if he has to."

Tafee stands up. She gathers her robe close around her. "He didn't before."

CAMP JOURNAL, 8.25.2145
@ CRETE, GEYSER

They reviewed the probe's footage and can determine nothing definite. The quality of light in the geyser is poor, but the temperature did increase the farther down the probe traveled.

I didn't realize you would be so real. I thought
this would feel less like cheating. But it doesn't.

Tafee Johanssen, recovered recording
8.10.2144 CE

8.26.2145

Aiya is tired in the morning, more than sleeplessness can
account for. She takes care in dressing, and she pins her
hair back close to her head. It is not customary for her to
pray outside of synagogue, and there is no synagogue in
the district, but she whispers, not to herself, "Please." She
looks around her small room. The bot is standing silent
in one corner. It blinks its red light and she chooses to
read it as encouraging. She wishes that she smelled eggs
cooking.

She is the last to arrive in the courtroom. Hertz is
alert, unlike yesterday. He is scribbling notes to himself

on his tablet. He barely looks up when she enters. 812-3 is standing at attention and she tries to see him anew, as she saw him the first time in the cell. What does he appear to be at first glance? As if that will put to rest her doubts. But she cannot rewind time. She reads into the set of his face, the thin line of his lips, anxiety.

"We're waiting for transmission," the clerk says. Her *robotnik* aide is not present this morning. Aiya wonders if her absence is related to the matter being decided today.

Aiya takes her place beside 812-3. The guards have not removed his wrist restraints. She glances at them and they ignore her. She notices that the captain of the military police is sitting at the back of the room, in the shadows of the corner. He winks at her, but it is not encouraging. She looks at 812-3 and smiles, taking a deep breath.

"Not long now," she says.

He turns his head to her. "She ordered me." His voice is barely even a whisper.

She bends closer. "What?"

He looks at his feet. "I did not want to remember it that way. But I think it is true now. I did not kill him. I did not want to kill him. Even if it was my hands."

She places a hand on his arm and wishes she could smile or express some sort of assurance. The clerk clears her throat.

"Incoming message," she informs them.

Aiya feels hot and cold all at once. The judges appear on the monitor. They look exactly as they did yesterday, down to the color of the pinstripes on their shirts. She glances at Hertz. He seems calm, his stance relaxed. The clerk is shuffling through papers of her own, forms not yet electronic even in space, uninvested in the moment.

The judges' formalities are brief.

"After examining the briefs provided by both appellant and appellee and after listening to the statements delivered yesterday, the court has come to a decision. We view the evidence of prejudice in the trial to be incontrovertible and, accordingly, we grant a new trial to Worker-class, ID 812-3, in the case of Colony, Europa v. Worker-class, ID 812-3."

The judge who has spoken looks down at the statement he is reading from and pauses. He looks at his female colleague, and she continues, elaborating on the decision of the court, naming precedents and references for the decision, and commenting on the implications for the future. Aiya knows this is what is happening. She can see the judge's lips move, but she can barely hear. Her ears are buzzing, and her blood is thumping.

812-3 sits down heavily beside her. The captain swears audibly from the back of the courtroom. Hertz slams his tablet on the table. None of them follow proper court decorum and the judges cannot see. They are all merely spectators.

812-3 opens his mouth to speak, but no words come out. It is the first time she has seen him at a loss. And though she is not sure she is his peer, he seems very human in that moment.

CAMP JOURNAL, 8.26.2145
@ CRETE, GEYSER

The ridge on which we have encamped shifted as we slept. There is some danger of losing our camp entirely if we do not move.

Members of the jury, the prosecution has rested its case on one thing and one thing only: that *robotnici* are not human, and anything not human must be capable of the most vile acts. But I will ask you a question: what is our precedent for understanding murder? For understanding theft or rape or abuse? Is it not something we have learned from each other?

Statement from the defense
Colony, Europa v. Worker-class, ID 812-3
6.24.2145 CE

8.27.2145

Aiya wakes up in her bed. Her head is foggy. The bottle of arak is open. She finds it with one hand dangling over the bedframe. A shot glass rolls across the tiles toward the door. She licks her teeth and her tongue is furry. She stumbles out of bed, into the bathroom, and she spits into the sink trying to clear her mouth. The drain sucks in the droplets of water. She hacks up mucus from her throat. "Mirror," she croaks. The wall becomes reflective in front of her. She pokes at the bags under her eyes. Her hair is bushy and she draws a hand through it half-heartedly. Then, she smiles. She remembers.

There is no backlog of trials in the district, so the Eta court scheduled the new trial less than a month from today. She promised she would visit 812-3 today and discuss strategy and approach. For the first time, *robotnici* would be included in the jury lottery. This, she told him, this would make all the difference. Alongside his willingness to introduce his memories into evidence.

In the kitchenette, she searches out a box of meal replacement bars, dense malt-flavored bricks. She slides into the stool at the counter inset into the wall. Her tablet is blinking with a collection of messages. There are threats and complaints from random Eta-assigned IPs, but also a few scattered congratulations. The names mean little to her. There is one, surprisingly, from Peri. The message is short and neutral, but not condemnatory. A pain around her chest, one she barely knew was there, eases a little.

There is also a message, with a video file attached, from the MP captain. She hovers over the thumbnail, anxiety pricking at the back of her neck. When she opens it, she realizes the message is disturbingly brief. It does not curse her out, it does not threaten her. It merely orders her to look at the attached video. The timestamp is from late the previous night, and it is a security feed from the prison. She feels suddenly sick. She drops the bar, and she pushes herself back from the counter. Maybe, she tells herself, maybe he is just taunting her with the video of the fight he showed her previously.

The bot is vainly trying to clean up the shot glass, pushing it like a ball across the room. It squeals in irritation, the noise of cracked belts. "Don't worry about it," she tells the bot, offhandedly. Her voice breaks. She swallows, trying to clear her throat. The bot stops moving. Its light blinks red, then yellow, then red.

She returns to the counter and stares at the message again. The captain's curses and Tafee's tears play, garbled and remixed, in her mind. For just a moment, she puts her hands over her ears as if that might block out the sounds. The sounds still. The apartment is quiet, so quiet that she can hear the others who live in this domicile moving in the hallway or adjoining apartments. There is nothing else she can do but play the video. She cannot turn her back on it or leave the apartment or take a shower.

In the video, 812-3 sits alone in the cafeteria, without

the guards or escort any sane warden would grant him in these circumstances, in the wake of a controversial hearing. She knows then. Without needing to watch anymore, she knows how the video will end. She presses one hand firmly over her stomach to calm herself and force herself to keep watching. Her other hand is over her mouth.

He is no longer wearing the borrowed suit. The striped jumpsuit makes his translucent skin and his white-blonde hair almost disappear. He is smart. He does not sit with his back to the room, but there is still space between him and the wall. The tables are grouped near the center of the room. When a group of prisoners approach him, some of them wearing bandages and casts, he stands up, ready for a fight. But he does not notice the woman who creeps behind him, pressed to the wall, a small knife or weapon grasped tight in her fist.

There are no guards in the room. The captain has made sure of that.

It is wrong to assume, as detectives Ghita and Ray did, that humans don't have the strength or viciousness to brutalize a person, to attack with savage abandon. Aiya knew this at the time she watched the footage of the crime scene at the drill, but she does not articulate it to herself until now, until just before the moment in which she watches the woman leap up onto 812-3's back and strike at his neck and spine, the only points of vulnerability in *robotnici* built for warfare and dangerous labor conditions.

812-3 does not crumple like a human under the pain and the assault. He stands open-mouthed and his eyes roll back into his head. The veins beneath his skin wink black and blue and then become pale and invisible. His arms drop to his sides and then his chin to his neck.

Aiya bites her knuckle, and the video ends with a roar from the crowded prisoners. The screen on her tablet goes dark. Her fingers move without thought, minimizing and then deleting the video. She opens the folders that hold her briefs, the records of the original trials, copies of the judges' messages from the appeal hearing. She deletes them, one after the other, each tokened by a tiny ping.

She can recover them if she wishes to, so it may be an empty gesture, but it is her instinct anyway.

She turns, numb and unthinking, and stoops to pick up the shot glass. She takes up the bottle of arak and she pours out a shot for herself. Head thrown back, she drinks it whole. The anise lingers on her tongue, the alcohol burns her throat. She imagines she is standing before a picture window, the glass orb of Europa suspended in front of her, and she curses it under her breath with every curse she knows.

CAMP JOURNAL, 8.27.2145
@ CRETE, GEYSER

The group has voted to return to the district before deciding a new place from which to camp and observe the geyser. I am to return with them, and I do not know if I will be chosen to come back to the geyser. In case of such an eventuality, I will visit the geyser myself in the early morning before we leave.

So she crossed the briny water from afar to Crete, beguiled by the wiles of Zeus.

Hesiod
Translated by Hugh G. Evelyn-White
1914

8.27.2145

It is dark in the room before Aiya comes back to herself. The bot is bumping against her foot in its eagerness to follow a trajectory under the bed and back again.

"Stop it," she says. Her voice is distant and strange to her, like someone else speaking. She kneels down and the bot freezes. Her fingers are clumsy and her mind is clouded with drink, but she searches over the top of the bot until she finds the panel she wants. She pries it up with her nails, rather than using the voice protocol. There is a small dongle and cable curled inside that she unweaves and plugs into her watch. The screen of the watch lights up with green lines of code. Remembering what she can of her rudimentary pre-settlement training, she searches for the word she wants.

"Here." She highlights a large block of code, the parameters of the bot's directive, relatively simple in one of its size. She deletes it. She is not an AI or software engineer, and she realizes after she has already done it that she cannot anticipate the result. For all she knows, she has just performed a lobotomy.

She stands back. Her bare feet are cold on the tile. The bot's lights blink through their available spectrum, red-yellow-green-blue-white, as its software attempts to function. The bot emits a series of high-pitched beeps, and Aiya glances up at her door, worried the neighbors might mistake it for an alarm. Then the bot goes still, and the lights turn off. It sits quiet. Aiya slumps back onto the bed, swallowing her disappointment and anger. She takes another shot of arak and falls back into sleep.

When she wakes, her watch tells her it is late at night. Curfew is long past and the artificial lights imitating moon and stars have long gone dark. Her window looks out onto blackness. When she checks the time, she also notices an extra file on her screen. It holds three temporary files, with video extensions. She thinks she might throw up, but she cries instead. She remembers the video files, 812-3's memories. Her body shakes and tears burn in her eyes. Her throat constricts and her face grows hot.

Think good things, Peri said as they exited the egg-like shuttles and saw the district laid out before them. She did not believe it, not really, even then, though she remembers smiling. The only good thing she can think of now is how she might still clear 812-3's name. *Name.* And she laughs out loud.

Eyes bleary, she looks at the door to her apartment. The bot is sitting there and now it is glowing, no longer using the lights embedded in its dome, but glowing yellow and warm from inside. "Out," it says, as if it knows she sees it.

She swings her legs out of bed and stumbles to the door. She presses her thumb to the keypad and the door slides open, whispering in the dark night. The bot slips out and pauses in the hallway as if considering which way to go. And where can it go, with checkpoints and locked doors and shuttle clearances combined? It picks a direction and rolls off, determination in the steadiness of its light and its unwavering course. She allows herself to imagine a happy ending for it, charging itself at solar stations, picking its way down the tunnels, ignored by those who expect to see the bot at work. Perhaps, in some abandoned corner of the Europan mines, it will find what the settlers have been looking for and it will not judge that alien life by human standards.

Perhaps.

The door slides shut. The life-support systems hum, checking temperature and oxygen as the room seals itself off from the outside. Aiya goes to her tablet. She recovers the files she deleted earlier, all of them—the videos of the hearing, the records of the first trial, her conversations with 812-3 in his cell. She does not open them or read them now. She powers down the tablet and she searches out her bed again.

But she will read them again in the morning, when the light, however artificial, is beating through her blinds.

CAMP JOURNAL, 8.28.2145
@ CRETE, GEYSER

I saw it as we left. It was the color of the ice.

Acknowledgments

Many thanks to the hardworking people at Tor.com Publishing, an imprint that is literally changing the way we view speculative fiction and has ushered in a golden era of novellas in our field. Especial thanks to my editor, Lee Harris, who has worked patiently with both me and the manuscript. The cover is gorgeous, so I also want to thank the artist, Will Staehle, and the designer, Christine Foltzer.

I also need to thank Aqueduct Press, the small feminist press that published my first book. It was affirmation that I was writing what I was meant to write.

My parents bought me my first boxed set of Lord of the Rings, so I feel it is partially their fault I do what I do. Enormous thanks and love to them and to my sister, who is an unfailing supporter of my work. My husband committed himself to a lifetime of peer review and editing, so I thank him as well.

And, of course, I am enormously grateful to my friends and colleagues in Ohio and New York (and the other states you've moved on to). You are an unparalleled support network.

About the Author

Photograph © Brian Church

ERIN K. WAGNER is an English professor in the SUNY system, an Appalachian transplanted to the Catskills. Her short stories have appeared in a variety of publications, including *Apex Magazine* and *Clarkesworld,* and her poetry has been published in *Abyss & Apex* and the *South Dakota Review.* Her first novella, *The Green and Growing,* was published by Aqueduct Press. For updates, visit her website at erinkwagner.com.

TOR · COM

Science fiction. Fantasy. The universe.

And related subjects.

*

More than just a publisher's website, *Tor.com*

is a venue for **original fiction, comics,** and

discussion of the entire field of SF and fantasy,

in all media and from all sources. Visit our site

today—and join the conversation yourself.